Signs of Life

Signs of Life

channel-surfing through '90s culture

**Edited by
Jennifer Joseph
and
Lisa Taplin**

manic d press
san francisco

© 1994 Manic D Press

Cover: Slatoff+Cohen

Distributed to the trade by PUBLISHERS GROUP WEST

Printed in the United States of America

5 4 3 2 1

Signs of life : channel-surfing through '90s culture / edited by
  Jennifer Joseph and Lisa Taplin.
      p.   cm.
   ISBN 0-916397-21-1 : $12.95
    1. Popular Culture--United States--Literary collections.
    2. American literature--20th century.   I. Joseph, Jennifer.
   II. Taplin, Lisa, 1969-
   PS509.P64S54 1994
   810,8'0054--dc20   94-30707
                                                         CIP

CHANNEL GUIDE

Signs of Life

DEEP IN THE HOUSE OF NOW
Kathi Georges

I like to dance. So I go to the discotheques, the dance halls, the raves.

My first rave. I hear about it from some paisley friends. They hand me a neon flyer that instructs me in rhyming couplets to call a certain phone number on the day. I call the number and, after punching in a secret code on my touch-tone phone, I get a voice mail message that says to drive to a certain corner between 9 and 11 p.m., and to recite a phrase from a popular Dr. Seuss book to a certain guy wearing a white turtleneck pullover.

At 9:45 I drive to the corner. It is in a dark part of town, brightened only by the light of a Colt 45 Malt Liquor sign inside the barred windows of a lonely corner market. A small crowd of drunk men in dark, stained clothing hover near the store's entrance, sharing a bottle of wine. They recite the standard phrases of lust upon seeing me in my purple bustier, orange overall shorts, pink polkadot tights and thigh-high lime green vinyl boots. I don't see anyone wearing a white turtleneck. Just as I am about to leave, I spot a fluorescent red poster stapled to a telephone pole. The poster reads, *Don't be foolish, don't be shy, with flowers in your hair, see the sky, see the sky.* I look up and see only dark windows. Then I grab some daisies from my dashboard, slap them in my hair, and look up again. A man in a white turtleneck leans out of a third-story window. I shout the passwords. He smiles and flashes a peace sign, then throws a paper airplane down at me that flies through my open car window and lands on the passenger seat. The drunks applaud and shout. One of them approaches my car, growling low. I speed away.

A block later, I pull over and unfold the paper airplane. In the dim glow of a penlight, I see more rhyming poetry, several references to *Alice in Wonderland*, and a map to an industrial part of town, with no address. I drive past abandoned buildings. Burnt out streetlights. Billboards that carry only peeling fragments of messages from five years ago.

I keep driving until I reach the area where the flyer said the rave would be. I park, stash my pull-out radio under the front seat and get out, searching for signs of life.

The sidewalk is cracked and broken. In some places, it disappears completely and my boots crunch on broken glass and dirt. Trash blows in low lazy circles: faded newspapers, cigarette butts, ripped pieces of old clothing. The wind whispers of dead dreams and time. I shiver, remembering what I want to forget. A rat saunters crookedly down the gutter.

And then I am there.

An old rundown warehouse made of rusting corrugated steel. A line of twenty people in brightly colored clothes. Singing. Skipping. Laughing.

I ask a fawn-eyed girl, "Is this where it's at?"

She giggles and exhales, "Where it's at is where you're at."

I get in line.

Inside: a dark lobby obscured by a big-bosomed smiling woman who takes a twenty dollar bill from me and throws it into a thirty-gallon plastic trash can. She stamps my hand with Cyrillic letters in red ink that she says spell 'Love'.

A pulse of distant music. Bright yellow happy faces hanging from the ceiling. Florescent arrows on every wall pointing ten directions.

Narrow, rickety stairs. Two topless women in leather boots strike poses at the top. More fluorescent arrows. The sound pulls me into the main room. I stand and stare.

Five hundred people. Five hundred smiles, lit by the diffused glow of flashing video projections. Fractal skulls merge with movie-star glamor stills, medical training montages and exploding ink blobs. Music penetrates visions of riot grrrls in short flower print dresses swinging madly from tires suspended from the ceiling. Shrieking and singing. Whirling and spinning.

A girl with long brown hair floats past carrying a large stainless steel bowl filled with pills and flowers. "Extra! Extra! Read all about it!" She gazes at me with invitation. I grab a flower and a pill. She chants, "Ten... Two for twenty... Three for twenty-five." I give her twenty and take another flower and pill. I swallow the pills and put the flowers in my hair.

Desdemona. Her name is Desdemona. I ask her about Shakespeare. She says she loves the Shakespeare Sisters, she read about them in the *Village Voice*. She squeezes my arm. Floats away.

The music throbs. I wander.

Another room. Darker. Calmer. White screens divide areas against the wall into small cubicles. I stare at a pastoral Japanese print on one of the screens. A tall boy walks up and whispers in my ear, "It's a global village thing." He disappears behind the screen. I follow.

Pillows. Smoke. Couples. I sit in a corner. The girl on the floor next to me has her head in the lap of a dark-haired young man wearing an oversized floppy velvet hat. She quietly sucks his cock. I glance at her. She looks up. Our eyes exchange universal understanding. I feel warm all over.

Back to the main room. The groove is there. Whirl and spin on cushions of air. The beat is everything. Presence. Now.

I see the girl and boy from the room. They smile.

We are on the floor. Sitting. Holding hands. Passing electricity. We lay down.

There is this moment and no other. There is peace and no other. There is love and no other. We are in the music. We are the music. We are all servants and masters. We are all in love. We are all happy. We are all.

Songs melt together. We dance. Sit. Swing. Laugh. Hug. Go to the cubicles. We know each other like old friends, young lovers. Everything is right and everything is now and now is as eternal as the beat in this dark room of smiles.

We are surprised, suddenly, by a different kind of light. Sunlight—shafting at sharp angles through half-painted panes of glass.

We recognize time and hesitate.

A spry fellow in Edwardian garb attempts to soothe us. "We shall continue our joy in the park!"

We stream down the narrow stairs to the sound of his bamboo flute.

The sharp blast of day separates. I look for familiar faces. They are there—still radiant—but distant. Hot shadows focus every flaw. Magic dissipates. I detach, alone.

Through the dirty streets I wander like the still drifting trash until I find my car. Someone has smashed the window and stolen the radio.

I brush broken glass off the seat and drive home, humming softly.

SOMETHING LIKE A RACCOON CALLED DULUTH ON THE MAXWELLS' PHONE
Steven Dean Pastis

It was a raccoon that broke into the Maxwells' home and ran up their telephone bill to an astronomic amount. Or so they told the lemon-scented woman at the counter of the telephone office.

"Really and truly, that's the way it occurred," maintained Mr. Maxwell, the brains of the family. "We don't know anybody in Duluth."

Mrs. Maxwell nodded, as did the three young Maxwells. The woman at the counter walked off in the general direction of her immediate supervisor. She decided to pass this problem along to someone paid to handle such things.

Selma was the supervisor at the office that day. She knew enough to find the Maxwell file and take it with her to the front counter and the waiting Maxwells.

"I find the story about the raccoon hard to believe," stated Selma to the Maxwell clan. "It says here that two months ago you told us that $430 in phone bills was attributed to a buffalo that snuck in through your kitchen window and called his brother in the Antelope Valley. December of last year you claimed that an antelope had knocked down your front door to make eight hours of calls to his nephew in Buffalo. And now this raccoon. How stupid do you think we are?"

Mr. and Mrs. Maxwell speculated on the stupidity level of the phone company staff without reaching an appropriate conclusion. The discussion returned to the raccoon situation after about five minutes.

"A raccoon could not have broken in your house and used the phone," explained Selma. "A raccoon would have immersed the telephone in water before having anything to do with it. The water would have rendered the telephone useless. Instead of a high phone bill, you people would be bringing in the telephone for repairs."

Mr. Maxwell thought for a moment.

"A badger. That's it. It was a badger that broke into our home and called Duluth," said the patriarch of the Maxwell family.

Selma thought for a moment and signed an approval for a refund for the calls to Duluth. The Maxwells were happy and went home. They were greeted by a mountain lion who was sitting in their kitchen talking to relatives in Saginaw.

"What do we do now?" asked one of the younger Maxwells of her equally concerned father. He thought for some time before bringing out his camera. A photograph might be needed for their next visit to the telephone company counter, and he would have that photograph.

"Some people are so suspicious," Mr. Maxwell thought to himself.

The photographs of the mountain lion came out so well that extra copies were sent to several magazines. The money from the magazines for use of the photos was used by the Maxwells to install bars on all the windows and extra locks on all of the doors.

After that, any animals wanting to use the Maxwells' telephone had to resort to extreme cleverness to get into the house. They dressed up as Girl Scouts selling cookies or more often as telephone repairmen. The Maxwells were pretty sharp and always seemed to be one step ahead of these would-be long distance telephone call makers.

One day, a reporter came by to do a story about the struggle of the Maxwell family against the members of the animal kingdom that sought to run up their telephone bills. Once inside the house, the reporter was attacked by the Maxwell clan who mistakenly thought he was a lynx.

The entire Maxwell family was sent to prison for the attack.

These days, the members of the animal kingdom are free to use the Maxwell telephone for calls to anywhere they want. No Maxwells are there to defend their home. But no animals come around. Somehow, it's just not fun anymore.

NARC
Ayn Imperato

I was reaching for a jar of pickles when I noticed him: the undercover cop at Safeway, disguised in a white *Try and Burn This One* American flag t-shirt and a red baseball cap, holding a long yellow sheet of paper with the words SHOPPING LIST emblazoned boldly across the top. He was so obvious it was laughable. He practically still had powdered donut dust around his collar. I knew he was a cop by the way he walked around like a wrestler, using his shoulders to propel himself forward, his fat arms sticking out from his sides like he had an orange stuffed under each armpit. That and the way he cruised by my aisle with his cart, again and again, glancing down at me, casual and bored. On his third pass I looked up at him and for a moment we locked eyes.

Swirling in those iron blue spheres were the stories of nabbed thieves: lowdown good-for-nothing out of work crooks and vagrants who stole bread and peanut butter and cans of peas because the hollow hunger in their bellies gnawed too impatiently to wait through fruitless hours of panhandling to feed their families and themselves. Nosiree. He'd gotten them all. Not one pocketed bagel or carrot-slipped-down-the-pants got past those automatic double doors with him overseeing the supermarket.

He pulled his cap down over his eyes and rolled on, trying to appear as anonymous as possible, continuing his casual gait back and forth. I knew that he was following me because I fit the suspicious character description in the Safeway Security Manual with my bright orange hair, nose ring, and black hooded sweatshirt with a frontal pouch fit for pocketing flat packages.

But it was something else too. Cops always follow me. Shit, you get caught shoplifting once or twice in your life and you wear it like a brand on your forehead. Deceit and trickery has a scent and cops can sniff you out like you wore thief cologne from a black bottle. They see the memory of the bars in your eyes. And they move in fast every time so you can never forget.

I had no intention of stealing. Just wanted to get a few groceries for the week, but I shrugged and figured I might as well have some fun.

Smirking, I pulled the hood of my sweatshirt over my head and shifted my eyes mischievously under my bangs, sort of bending over my cart a little to look as suspicious as possible, and I stalked to the end of the aisle to a pyramid of stacked up cans.

There I fingered through the special on creamed corn, laboriously reading each label and shaking each can to check for the proper amount of liquidity, as the Incredible Hulk briskly shuffled through slabs of wrapped meat behind me, reading and flipping through each one like they were books. I wondered how long I could get him to rummage through the meats.

I whistled as I read. Water. Corn Kernels, Milk, Salt, Calcium Phosphate (a preservative to retain color and flavor). I thought of the first time I got caught shoplifting. I was eleven, bored and poor. Mom wasn't around during the afternoon, and Dad was merely a memory. So I was in Woolworth's at the local mall, fingering plastic fruit earrings when I noticed these Shawn Cassidy clip-ons. They were huge hot pink discs with his face embossed in full color on the front and I knew I had to have them. Shawn Cassidy was the raddest, with hair so feathered the two sides touched in the back. I could never get my hair to stay like that, trying as I did in front of the upstairs bathroom mirror, and succeeded only in frying the hairspray stiff pieces into two frizzy masses on the sides of my face. So I didn't have any money. I never had any money, and there was Shawn

Cassidy glittering at me on the rack. So I slipped the earrings up my gauze sleeve and made immediately for the exit so I could lose myself amongst the crowds of summertime mall shoppers in flip-flops and halter tops.

The big hand circled around my arm and fastened itself like a lock, just as my body merged with the outside crowd. I was so close I could taste my escape in my throat. My chest pounded furiously. I instantly thought of kicking his knee in, but when I turned around and saw the size of him, I knew any effort would be fruitless.

"Get back here, you little shit," he hissed and I glanced down at his red plastic rent-a-cop name tag next to his aluminum badge.

"You got me, *Bill*," I snarled, looking up at him. His neck turned beet-red and then all I could see as he screamed at me was his enlarged Adam's apple bobbing up and down like a fat yo-yo in his throat.

He pulled me back in the store and led me like a limp doll through the aisles to a doorway in the back of the store. Inside was an ordinary office, which didn't look as treacherous as I had imagined from the outside. It was a green wallpapered room with one small window overlooking the mall parking lot. It looked and felt like being in the principal's office and, feeling in more familiar surroundings, I calmed down a bit. The cop sat me down across a desk from him. I stared blankly as he talked at me and his words blew through my skull like a thick breeze. I just sat there staring at that lump in his throat jumping up and down like a toy.

There was a buzzing silence. That apple in his throat hovered mid-neck.

"Well?" he said. "Are you going to give them up, or am I going to have to take them from you? I watched you hide them up your sleeve. I know you have those earrings. You're caught. You're *fucked*."

That was a way the principal had never put it, but I knew I was clean busted. I glared at him for a moment. Then fished around my sleeve and brought them out. I threw the discs across the desk and they clattered across to his knuckles. He kept his fingers still for a moment, then lifted his eyes up at me and grabbed them up in his hand.

"We at Woolworth's have a strict shoplifting policy. Don't be a brat," he warned. "Do what I say and this will be much easier on the two of us. I'm not enjoying this, you know."

"Can you just call my mom so I can get out of here?" I sighed.

He paused. "What do you think this is, Junior High School? This is the real world, *baby*, and I could call the cops on you right this minute. I could throw you in Juvie for five months for this. I could screw you for life."

I looked down at my green gauze blouse. My fingers were twisting the ends of the material in knots

"Look," he continued, sighing. "Why'd you take them? They're only 49¢ earrings, for Christ sake."

"I don't have any money. My mom doesn't have any money."

"Oh," he said. It was quiet for a moment and the overhead fluorescent lamp buzzed.

He asked for my mom's phone number and I gave him her work number. As we waited for her to show, we sat together in the office. He sat there, squat, shuffling papers around on the desk, and myself sitting motionless, staring out the one tiny window at cars pulling in and out of spaces in the parking lot outside.

An hour and a half later Mom's face, blond and haggard through the thick cheap makeup, popped through the door.

"Let's go," she said to me, and thanked the cop so profusely she practically slobbered on his shoes.

"Doin' my job," he said. Then he turned to me. "Look out there, little lady. I hope you've learned something today."

"Yeah," I said. "Don't get caught." And Mom yanked me through the door.

As we walked across the parking lot to the bus stop on the corner, she ignored me with a cold silence. From behind her, I watched her chunky body waddle in her green polyester dress. It still had that stain on the butt from the time she sat on a dollop of ketchup at Denny's.

Sitting on the bench at the bus stop, she finally spoke. She shook her head. "Oh, Kathleen," she sighed. "How could you embarrass me like that?"

I looked at her but she wouldn't look me in the face. I watched her stare off into traffic shaking her head, big tears welling up in her mascara-encrusted eyes. I stared down at my palms thinking of how I wished my hands had brains too, so they wouldn't snatch up pretty things. The bus came and she never mentioned it again.

The disguised supermarket cop was still shuffling through the meats, though he had moved on to fondling the chickens. I turned my cart around suddenly and took off, wheeling away fast down the linoleum. He casually followed, glancing sideways, but I weaved in and out of the aisles and stacked displays until he lost sight of me. I stopped in the prepackaged dessert section to catch my breath. My eyes focused on the macaroons, waiting for him to catch up to me. One brand of cookies had a series of president cards enclosed in each package, visible through the cellophane. I pushed feverishly through the crinkling packages, searching for Nixon. Five minutes later, just as I had found him and put the card with Richard's fleshy face in my pocket, the cop rounded the corner. I looked up at him, nonchalantly pricing a bottle of Clamato down at the other end of the aisle.

Chuckling, I rolled slowly away around the corner to the paper goods section, with him steadily behind. I stopped and lingered at the feminine hygiene section and I knew I had him good. He glanced around nervously under his baseball cap as he scanned the aisle. I mean how long could he pretend to look for Tampax for his girlfriend before some of the other customers would start to look at him funny? I rummaged through the array of cardboard boxes, pretending to slip one in my sweatshirt pocket, then taking it out again. I held up a jumbo box of pads so I knew he could see. He blushed and strode past me to check out the toilet paper and I laughed. He disappeared and I got bored, so I followed him to the produce section.

He was fingering the watermelons when he caught sight of me, picked up the bait again and rolled closer towards me.

The second time I got caught for shoplifting was two years ago, before I got a job at the bakery that I slave at now. I had just turned eighteen and was staying with my friend Vanessa. I stole a small radio because I had never had one of my own before. This time a puny cop in a baggy uniform and soggy hands caught me in an electronics store. Before I could punch him out, he slapped handcuffs on my wrists. But instead of calling my mom, they took me to jail.

They did call my mom later from the holding office, but she never came down to get me. I didn't blame her, and I knew she didn't have the cash to blow anyways. So three hours later I had to call Vanessa. She pulled together some cash and bailed me out, but it took her two days.

While I waited for her to save me, I sat in the holding cell, looking at my hands and up at the thick bars, with ten other women—hookers, thieves, and junkies—all standing, pacing, and slumped against the wall around me. For a moment the bars looked like thin black ribs and I felt swallowed inside the concrete walls. I knew I would see them again and again because life was boring and unfair and I would never get what I wanted without having to work my ass off for it.

I glared at the cop across a mountain of apples, giving up the facade. He surveyed the cabbages and turned a bundle of celery over in his hands again and again, but he wouldn't look up at me and let down his act. He strolled around rummaging through vegetables, with all the time in the world, searching for the perfect onion or turnip. He was good, but I was better. When no one was looking, I reached over and with a sweep of my arm caused an avalanche of potatoes. He looked up at me and I twisted my cart around fast and made for the bakery, hiding behind the trees of French loaves in the bins. When the cop came towards me again, I moved towards the checkout lines.

From my line, I looked up and saw traces of a commotion around the mess in the produce stands, and a few escaping potatoes rolling away on the linoleum. I felt sorry for doing it when I saw a haggard employee in a dirty white apron helplessly scooping them up in his arms.

As I unloaded my cart onto the conveyor belt, I looked over at the cop at the checkout lane at the far end near the door, where I knew he would be, pretending not to know all the cashiers by name. I paid for my things, hefted the paper bag of groceries and made my way to the exit. On my way to the automatic doors, I moved in extra close as I walked in front of him. I reached in my pocket and handed him the Nixon card, face up. I leaned in as I passed him, and whispered, *"Narc."*

LAST NIGHT
Jeffrey McDaniel

There was a knock at 1:34.
The woman living above me
said she had to be up at 6,
asked me to stop
thinking about my family.

I apologized, decided to clean
a week's worth of dishes in an hour.
As I scraped ketchup sludge
from the cracks in a plate,
a man across the street began yelling:

Put a sock in it, you
long-haired ding-dong,
you're waking up the neighborhood.
Your mother never loved you!

I closed the window,
poured a thick tongue of whiskey
over the silence of ice cubes
and shook the glass like a throat.

A wine bottle busted the window,
cradling the voice of an alley drunk:
You treated your younger brothers like shit,
you selfish schlock, fill this up.

I pissed in the bottle's lips
and lobbed it to the darkness, re-arranged
my posters, changed my socks,
when there was a tap at the bedroom window.

The owner of the bar downstairs
crouched on the fire escape:
My customers can't hear the music, mac.
Here's a hundred bucks,
get a few drinks and a whore.

I grabbed him by the lobes and screamed,
listened to those tiny ear bones rattle,
when the phone rang. It was the mayor:

You missed your grandmother's birthday
again. Not even a phone call
after all she's given you.

That's it, I said, I'm leaving this city,
when a voice bullhorned:
This is the chief of police, son.
We know all about how you stole
your father's movie projector
and watched your older brother take the rap for years.

I ran up the stairwell, hollering:
So what if I did!
Kicked open the roof door,
found my grandfather in his old chair.
He offered me a cigarette.

I never told your father I loved him.
I never kissed the sweat
from your grandmother's neck.
It's too late for me,
but you got more time than a clock, boy.

Then he was gone.
I sat in the chair he left behind,
stared over the skulls of rooftops,
lonelier than the last tooth
in the mouth of a dead man.

Degenerate creeps,
monsters who leap~
On every corner: more danger.

Duck drive-by shootings
and gangs who're looting~
& never take sweets from a stranger.

If you don't stay alert,
you're sure to get hurt.
Perverts eat miniskirt flirts
for dessert!

So inside let us hide,
to avoid homicide.
We'll cower behind furniture.

If we never go out,
then, without a doubt,
we can always be safe & secure.

the end

PHLOX
OR
WHY MEN NEVER HAVE ENOUGH GUNS
Dean Kuipers

Ben eats some eggs and reaches into the open case behind him to crack open a summer-hot Point Beer. We got the Stooges on the box drowning out the cicadas thanks to me, cos I hid the only tape Ben has listened to for days, The Smiths' *Hatful of Hollow*. I worked all week for a roofer with that pitiful drone in my head and I can't believe I didn't fall off a barn or get hit by lightning or something. Ben moves his plate aside and picks up this oily bundle he brought down for breakfast. The thing's been laying under his cot in the attic for almost a week and we'd all been dyin to ask. He pulls rubber bands off the bundle and unwraps a towel from around it, starts talking for the first time in two and a half days.

"These vintage Colt revolvers can be made new from kits," he says, holding up a huge, oily six-shooter freshly hatched in the watery-blue light of morning. "Me and my dad made this one when I was home from school one summer."

Suddenly he is very young, twenty years old from the suburbs of Detroit with a streak of melancholy that sends him out in the mornings into the foot-high corn, where he hunches down on a little hillock and stares at the Red River. He travels with a few bottles of prescription dope. He's willing to share it.

"It comes all milled but unassembled," he says, "like the casings and the barrels are all milled and numbered but there's no shine. The wood's just blocks. You got to do some light machine work on some of the parts to get 'em to fit."

He opens a tool box and starts cleaning the gun.

I got two shotguns and a rifle at home, so I say, "Thing looks perfectly clean to me."

He gives me a severe look. "You have to clean it every day. Cos rust kills people. Yeah. Rust will kill ya."

The odor of solvent and gun oil fills the leaky old cabin. Makes the eggs taste great, like we're up in the Yukon in Jack London days.

But it's the dead of summer in a lost corner of inland Wisconsin, a four-corners named after a tiny field flower called Phlox. Watchin' Ben clean the gun, wondering why he brought it here.

All night this tiny barn-bat tried to land on the brass rail of the tarnished headboard on my bed, about a foot and a half above my face, and all night it missed. In the airless roar of insects I'd sense it there above all four of our beds and hear the soft click of its nails, the tiny screech as it slowly lost a grip on the rounded brass and slid off, then a chip and a scree as it took the air again to make another pass. The other fifty bats living in the wall would rustle and scree back at it.

All the beds were shared and a woman shared mine, a woman I hardly knew but after one night we both agreed it was way too hot to wear pajamas and we went to bed naked and it had become a routine that all night she would reach over and softly ply my lazy penis, start in on it again like it was a rosary, and all night I'd say no and kiss her once to let her know it wasn't a big rejection. No to her cinderblock swimmer's body, big shoulders slinging the sheets off us and powerful naked hips arching up against the batty darkness. I could smell her dyin to get off. And I said no cos I was evil. Cos I wanted to prove to her that I was the toughest twenty-one-year-old man she'd ever bedded, and I could prove it, and in three months we never once made it, and she knew I wasn't queer and it hurt her, bad. I needed some power then and this was the cheapest power I could get.

Ben slept on a cot next to us. With the Colt underneath.

"Y'all sure are quiet," Ben says to me, cleaning the gun, jerks his head toward the attic so I know he means me and the swimmer.

"Oh, I suck a tit or something but that's about as far as it goes, Ben," I whisper. "I'm not gonna take it just cos it's layin there."

He nods.

"Why don't you try?" I say. "Get me out of a jam." He didn't have too many girlfriends.

"Oh, shit. Can't do that," he says. He seems irritated by the suggestion so I dropped it. He has the gun.

I clean some dishes and get beer and find Ben out in the orchard on his knees. Nate comes out and we lean against the ancient trees, too old and neglected to bear anything but stone-hard little apples and peaches and plums, untended since Nate's grandpa died decades back.

The revolver is a model that pre-dated brass cartridges. You load each chamber by hand. Ben rests the butt on a cloth, measures black powder into all six chambers from a leather bag, sets a rough, huge .45 caliber lead ball into each and tamps it down with a set of calipers. Then he smears the ends over with what looks like Crisco.

"This stuff keeps the fire from jumping from one chamber to the next. I'd hate to have it chain-fire. All six go off at once. These two chambers that can't get out right there would probably kill ya, blow your arm off anyway. The rest, who knows where they'd go? Into something or someone."

Nate gets behind a tree. It isn't the gun itself he's afraid of and Ben knows it.

Ben spins the cylinders and flips it into place with a little Steve McQueen action, then puts it down and fishes around in his tackle box and comes up with some plastic McDonaldland characters to use as targets. They're little, each one about three inches tall.

"Perfect," I say. "Blow the hell outta Mayor McCheese."

Ben chuckles at that and seems genuinely pleased with himself, toddles off in his cardboard-new Oshkosh overalls he bought on the drive north, and sets these little plastic dudes all along the side of a hill in the orchard. He's still chuckling when he walks back, breathes, picks up the gun and turns without really aiming or blinking or thinking or flinching or reacting to the booming recoil and puts a hole in all except one from about twenty yards. I was watchin *High Plains Drifter*. He's a natural.

He stops, sucks the smoke out of the gun, says, "I like that smell," and reloads it for me and Nate. He goes on shooting until lunch, cleans the gun, then shoots all afternoon. He's got bags and bags of supplies. This goes on for days. The orchard looks like it's been chewed over by a rabid mole.

A few nights later I'm watching Ben clean the gun for the third time that day, slowly, meticulously, by lamplight at the kitchen table. Nate and his girl and the swimmer are laughing out on the doorstep in the night, smoking these crude cigars called backwoods smokes to keep the mosquitoes off.

The Colt opened Ben up a little bit. He isn't going back to college in the fall. He quit. He came back from a year in Africa and dyed his hair orange. He fears the suburbs and his parents' home and he wants a more permanent freedom ticket. He uses those words together: *permanent freedom*. My power trip with the swimmer is fizzling and our friends from Kalamazoo blow in and out with unintelligible agendas and I waver for a moment, scared, thinkin that only the crumbly, bug-eaten walls of this cabin keep all our insides from pouring out into the soil like so much lead shot, so much spent talent, so much good aim practiced and practiced just to blow the head off a plastic Hamburglar.

"Last chance for some of these meds," he says suddenly, wrapping up the gun. "I'm not taking them anymore. I haven't been taking them the whole time we've been here. I'm throwin 'em out."

Three weeks later. Ben has a job at a bakery in Detroit, five–six hundred miles away, says he hates it, demands a week off and gets it and drives all night to the cabin. Gets there weirdly fresh, looking like he just rolled out of bed and shower. It's blistering hot. Tells us that he can't stand it if baking dinner rolls is what his life's become. We get up in the morning, he's gone and the corn's too high to see him anymore. I yell for him out in the fresh-cut hayfield that butts up to the cabin but there's no answer so I just stop.

I'm in the Phlox General Store looking for some mail and Nate's up on the levy of Phlox Pond playing guitar. I stop over to the gas station to look again at a pink '51 Buick in mint condition sittin there for sale, just like I do every time we go to the store. Ben drives by.

He drives up the dirt road past the horseshoe pits and the turn-off for the softball field and parks on the edge of the pond, not far from Nate. Doesn't even say hi. Bends into the car and pulls out a harmonica, puts it on the roof. Stands there occupied by something in the middle of the pond.

Huge cumulus zeppelins stack up in the electric tedium of summer. Fat clouds of algae and reflections of clouds rush together at the last minute over Phlox Pond toward the little floodgate and become the Red River beneath Nate's feet. Ben just stands there like he's ready to dive in and I think he's gonna then he bends into the car again and comes out with the Colt and I start walking a little faster down the road. Nate's just sittin' there on the levee, looking over at Ben and changing the fingering on the guitar and singing with a mockingbird, I don't think he can see the gun from where he's at, but then Ben makes that little Steve McQueen wrist-flip again that he only does when it's loaded and I hear the cylinder snap into place even though I'm still a hundred yards down the road, and Nate puts his guitar down softly on the gravel and I break into a run and Ben takes the Colt by the wrong end, by the barrel, holds it up by his chest and neither one of us even gets time to shout ... as he wheels ... like an axe-thrower at the fair ... and sends the gun booming high out over the pond, I didn't know he had that kind of arm, and it hangs there ... menacing everything, fully able to tear a giant hole in all things living, and then just sploots into cold, rusty-green spring water, barely rippling the clouds.

A heifer's bawling out across the pond. I pull up short, sweat running instantly down the crack of my ass. We all look at the pond like you'd expect it to show, somehow, the water should change color or a huge muffled explosion should burp up from the depths or the clouds should race by like a movie—nothing happens. No trace. Nate, he has it so wired, he just sits down and starts playing the same song again, seeing the harmonica on the car all along. Ben puts the tackle box in the car, picks up the harmonica, says hi to me with a big grin, then tries to play along to the song, but it's hard for him to make smooth notes cos he's got a bad case of the shakes.

A BLAZE OF GLORY
Keith Dodson

A walkie-talkie
rides my hip
its staccato bursts
checkerboard
the night
I
walk the polished hall see
myself a Swat Team commander
directing an assault see
myself a Fire Chief
controlling a five alarm fire see
myself an Army Sergeant
adjusting artillery
to save his platoon
when my co-worker
two buildings down squawks up,
"Ya got any toilet paper
over there?"
and I see
myself a middle-aged custodian
tugging a walkie-talkie
from his belt
just to
say,
"No."

THE PARADISE LOUNGE
Kurt Zapata

I went to a poetry reading a while ago at the Paradise Lounge. My friend Jim promised it was better than sitting home on a Sunday night watching TV, you know, being live entertainment and all. I was skeptical (not really thinking I was the poetry type), but the price was right: free. We decided to meet inside and check it out.

I remember thinking to myself as I walked in, "Poetry, huh? This should be pretty tame."

But I'm here to tell you: Bad Luck and Trouble follow me around like bored little brothers.

Well anyway, I showed up about ten minutes late for the poetry reading (which was probably a good thing, meant I missed about ten minutes of it). Immediately, I noticed one thing about poets: they carry around way too much paper with them. You'd think that being the educated, politically correct, poetry types they would try to conserve paper in these environmentally trying times and all, but no. Everyone had seven or eight sheets spread out in front of them like they were gonna break out in verse at any given moment. Even from the back of the room, where I like to stand, I could hear people drop buzz words like *tonality, commitment,* and *work-in-progress,* in between names.

Holy smokes, I knew I was in for a literate experience.

Well, it was obvious I was late because the featured Poet-Guy was already on. Now I don't want to sound like some sort of a poetry snob or connoisseur or something (hell, my taste is in my mouth) but in my opinion this guy was no good. He stood in the cliché Poet-Guy stance: one leg forward, weight on the back leg, head held slightly aloft, arm cocked; the whole nine yards. He even had on a turtleneck sweater. A white one. It grated my nerves to no end.

I mean, Poet-Guy was really full of himself. He had these insipid voices for the characters in his poems. I swear. Well, actually to his credit, one of them sounded like Mr. Whoopee from the old *Tennessee Tuxedo* cartoon. And worse yet, Poet-Guy kept mentioning his book over and over and over, like we were gonna rush out after the reading and buy it at our nearest all night bad poetry store.

He started one poem with, "This is dedicated to the woman who published my book...," and another with, "This is from my book...," I consciously forgot the title. Anyway, as if this wasn't enough, his poetry was loaded with these huge, obscure words. It got to the point where I couldn't figure out what the fuck Poet-Guy was talking about.

I don't know, call me stupid, but "Vermilion cuneiform reptiles issue forth from my delineated mind," just didn't do anything for me. In fact, it seemed to me that Poet-Guy was trying to demonstrate his mental superiority to the rest of us dim slobs. Like we should be jealous of his iron-fisted grasp on the English language. Several were the times Poet-Guy began on a lengthy, indecipherable, free-form tangent and I found my mind wander off to more immediate, mundane thoughts:

"Should I try to shoulder my way through the crowd at the bar for another beer?"

"Man, that girl across the room sure has on a stupid looking hat."

"I hate the Poet-Guy's turtleneck sweater; needs a drink spilled on it." You know, just those typical, random, bored type of thoughts that pop up unexpectedly as your eyes sweep the room. I guess the crowd felt the same way because they turned ugly.

These three girls in the front had lost all interest and were talking among themselves, trying to drown out Poet-Guy. Regardless, he went on.

The rest of the crowd began to heckle Poet-Guy. I couldn't believe it, because that seemed like a really fucked thing to do to someone who had the guts to stand up in front of a room full of strangers and read his bad poetry out loud, but I had to hand it to them; Poet-Guy deserved it.

"Yeah, yeah, yeah..." a girl to my left called out.

"It's got a point, right?" asked someone sarcastically. I turned around and headed towards the bar for a beer.

"Wrap it up!" came a male voice behind me.

Poet-Guy must have taken the last heckler's advice seriously because he announced he was done. A couple of people in the crowd clapped distractedly as he gathered up his papers and walked off the little two-inch high stage. Turning from the bar, I was treated to a view of Poet-Guy storming up, as his bad-poetry-lovin' girlfriend ran over in awe. She hugged him and said something to the effect of, "You were great, honey," proudly in some unintelligible European accent.

Poet-Guy couldn't even be honest with himself. "It had its highs and lows," he answered.

I asked the bartender for a beer, feeling slightly sickened. Poet-Guy pushed his way up to the bar and ordered two conciliatory drinks, paying with the chips he had received in compensation for his performance. Being kinda curious as to what Poet-Guy was drinking, I hung around for a second at the bar. Brown liquor over ice in a couple of hefty sized glasses. I went back to where a couple of friends of mine were standing.

Soon enough the next poet came on. They announced her as Terri White or Weiss or something like that, I didn't really catch her name but she was pretty good. At least she felt and meant everything she said, it wasn't just an exercise in mental masturbation meant to humiliate the rest of us. Terri was really into it and for that I respected her.

It worked well enough for the crowd because they quieted down. One of Terri's last poems was titled, *Bike Messenger Leads The People,* or something like that but I'd already had a couple of beers by then. Anyway, "Burn it Down!" was her theme because she kept screaming it out every couple lines, her back arched, hands clenched, eyes screwed shut.

Suddenly, right in the middle of it, some asshole slurs out, "Burn it

Down!" at the top of his lungs like some sort of drunken, tardy parrot.

"Oh well," I remember thinking to myself, "The crowd grows restless."

Another "Burn it Down" blurts out right behind me and when I turn to see who it was spitting in my ear, lo and behold, it's the Poet-Guy. Only he must have sucked down those two huge doses of liquid courage because now he's Drunken-Angry-Poet-Guy.

I couldn't fucking believe it. He'd just gotten heckled off the stage and here Poet-Guy was doing the same thing to somebody else. I mean, if someone hurt you, why would you turn around and become just like them? I guess it was part of that If-You-Can't-Beat-Em-Join-Em, Spread-The-Grief-Around sort of mentality that I love so much.

So anyway, now I've got Drunken-Angry-Poet-Guy behind me, draped over his Euro-babe, hurling out abuse from the safety of the back of the room. Every time he screamed out some insult, they would lurch forward and stumble into me. Let me tell you, Euro-babe was digging it, giggling all the while.

After about the fifth time he had screamed out some stupid comment and they'd slammed into me, I was about to tell this dork, "Hey look, I ain't no Aladdin's Lamp. Quit rubbing up against me." Well, right about then Terri announced she was finished and mercifully, Drunken-Angry-Poet-Guy fell silent.

After a ten minute break, it was open mike and people were allowed to come up and read one poem each. They were about on par with the rest of the evening, some better than others. One thing bothered me though; everyone just walked up, meekly read their poetry and stepped off. I couldn't see going out like that. If I was up there, I'd want to rattle their cages, tell the audience how much I hated nose rings, scream at them. Anything for a response other than that bored, polite smattering of applause. Anyway, at key moments in each poem the Drunken-Angry-Poet-Guy would offer his keen and witty insight. At least they seemed keen and witty to him but he was fucked up. And each time they would crash into me.

Finally, I turned around and considered punching him right in his fucking fat face. Wipe that smug grin right off his intellectually superior head. (You know, spill a little blood on that virgin turtleneck sweater).

Well, about then this blonde in one of those trendy, leopard skin, pill box type hats that are so hip nowadays, walked up to read her poem. It was this really twisted tale of growing up in an Italian-American family. All about her mother losing her virginity to a family relative, her own father's and brother's sexual advances and the family's refusal to talk about any of it, all tied up in this shifting psycho-babble.

Drunken-Angry-Poet-Guy yelled out some pretty stupid shit but I was too lost in Twisted-Poetry-Girl's tragic childhood experiences to really notice. It was pretty cool, let me tell you. Afterwards, the crowd cheered (they like a little blood) and Twisted-Poetry-Girl walked off. Right then, this little old lady who was near me, exploded. I mean to say she was irate, livid, hysterical and three or four other adjectives I can't come up with at the moment, but mostly hysterical.

The Hysterical-Old-Lady was about forty-five or fifty, a shock of dark hair peppered with gray, glasses, maybe 4'11" and eighty pounds. Now the Hysterical-Old-Lady'd been sitting through two hours of bad poetry and had about all she could stand. She leapt up and screamed "Bigot!" into Twisted-Poetry-Girl's face as she tried to pass by.

Twisted-Poetry-Girl didn't know what the fuck to say to the Hysterical-Old-Lady who was blocking her path.

"Finally, confrontation," I thought to myself. Something I could really get into. It was great, I had front row seats and the events unfolded right before my very eyes.

The Hysterical-Old-Lady screamed, "You bigot!" again and yanked Twisted-Poetry-Girl's poem out of her hands, wadded it up and threw it on the ground.

Twisted-Poetry-Girl's eyes bugged out. "Hey look, lady, I was born into this," she finally managed to stammer.

"Every time I come here," the Hysterical-Old-Lady shrieked, "all I hear is bigotry." And with that she reached out and tore this string of trendy hippie beads from around Twisted-Poetry-Girl's neck.

"Fuck yeah!" I thought to myself. "Let's beat up the poets!"

I turned around and looked for Drunken-Angry-Poet-Guy. This was it. I was going to punch him right in his fucking mouth. Get a couple of good shots in and maybe a kick or two while he was down. Teach him a good lesson about feeling superior and heckling people. Adrenaline O.D.

Unfortunately, all I caught was a glimpse of Drunken-Angry-Poet-Guy's back as he and Euro-babe disappeared down the stairs. "He who hesitates..." is the moral of that story.

Well, the best part of this whole sordid tale was, my friend Miles was on stage ready to do his thing, and during all the scuffling he kept repeating into the mike, "Excuse me, this is Poetry, not Performance Art, you'll have to leave."

So right on cue the bouncers came. Two huge Nirvanabe's with ponytails and leather jackets but they didn't know what the fuck to do. How could they bounce the Hysterical-Old-Lady?

They tried to grab her arms to escort her out but that made the Hysterical-Old-Lady all the more hysterical. By then she was kicking, squirming and screaming. Shit, I didn't think anyone could get that wound up over bad poetry.

Boy, was I wrong.

So finally, they got a grip on her and dragged the Hysterical-Old-Lady out. It was great; definitely the climax to the show. In retrospect, it turned out to be a pretty cool evening but I got to see something pretty unexpected: violence at a poetry reading.

HATING EACH OTHER
Hal Sirowitz

My therapist said that life consists of ups & downs.
She said that when you're down you don't believe
that life is worth living, but as soon as
you become involved in an "up" situation,
you realize that life is worth holding on to.
But when I mentioned what she said to a friend,
he said that she was wrong, that life
wasn't a math formula where one experience
could cancel out the other. And I was suddenly
faced with a dilemma. Who was smarter,
my therapist or friend? She said that he was
too emotionally involved with my life, & when
I felt sad, that made him sad. He said
That I pay her too much, & I could get
the same advice from a horoscope column.
I told her what he thought about her advice.
And she told me that even if he were her patient,
she could never cure him, because he had too many problems.
They liked hating one another, & if it wasn't
for me, they'd never have known about each other.

WIRED FOR MATE
Bucky Sinister

"We're back with our next guest, Jasper Whitewall. Jasper is the current Wirechess champion of North America, here in San Francisco to defend his title. For the few of you who don't follow Wirechess, Jasper has been the champion for three years." The camera angle widened to include the man sitting beside the speaker. "Jasper, how do you feel you will fare against your opponent?"

"Well, Steve, I have confidence that I will be representing the United States in the World Finals next fall. My opponent lacks the experience and intestinal fortitude necessary for the sport."

"So you are of the opinion that Wirechess is a sport?"

"Steve, anyone who has ever played Wirechess at a pro level knows the risks involved. One can get seriously hurt. It's one thing to play amateur with the external jacks, but once you make the brain conversions, the game becomes extremely brutal at times," Jasper said calmly.

"What about the claims that Wirechess is faked?" Steve asked.

"Look, if you don't believe the CAT scans, fine," replied the champion. "Look at Harvey Winchell's career. He left a trail of babbling idiots where geniuses once were, before he was banned from competition and disappeared. You think all those pros would fake insanity forever?"

"Assuming the damage is real, don't you think the possibility of being mentally injured should be lowered?"

"Steve, this is a game for the intellectual greats of our time. We know what we're getting into. If you took those possibilities away, there would be no way we could fill the Cow Palace tonight. People are out to see severe brain damage."

"Okay, we're getting low on time here." The host glanced at his notes on the desk in front of him. "Jasper, you're going to be at the Cow Palace tonight, pitted against Lisa Rivera from the Dominican Republic. Actually, by the time the home viewers see this, it will be over, correct?"

"Yes, it may still be in progress. You can catch it on Pay-Per-View," Jasper added.

"Okay, thanks for coming." Steve turned to face another camera. "We'll be right back with a man who claims to be Elvis reincarnated."

After taping for *Up With Steve*, Jasper Whitewall had the taxi let him off at a small cafe. He had about two hours to kill until he had to leave for the Cow Palace. He needed to sit and get his thoughts together before the match.

Rivera had induced a second personality in the previous Caribbean champion. It was the most horrid match he'd seen since watching Harvey Winchell as a teenager.

"I would like a double decaf mocha, please," Jasper said to the blond ponytailed person behind the counter who looked to be about seventeen. He was switching the music on the stereo, and appeared not to notice.

"Hey, you got a customer up here," Jasper yelled.

"Well, stall him for me will you, I'm busy," the ponytail muttered without looking around.

"Get up here and serve me, I haven't got all day."

The young man waited until he was done with the stereo and came up. "What did you want?"

"A double decaf mocha. I already told you," Jasper fumed.

"Look, don't make my life any more difficult than it needs to be by copping an attitude, okay?" he scolded motherly, going to work on the drink. The music kicked in. Jasper hated the music more than he despised the kid.

"What is this garbage? I don't think it's conducive to the dining atmosphere."

"First of all, the band's name is Ezra's Bad Habit. Secondly, this is a cafe, not a restaurant," he sneered, sliding the drink to him. "Two fifty."

"I don't like you. I can get you fired. I'm a very important man," Jasper threatened.

"I'll be careful. Now take your coffee and sit down."

Jasper was shocked. All he could do was give the guy his money and sit down. He took a table in the back and lit a cigarette. He thought about countering Rivera at her own game. She's too young, he thought, to have seen the master play. Harvey Winchell, you were the best. Well, second best. He snickered out loud and was reminiscing nicely when the smell of a litterbox interrupted him.

He looked up to see a greasy, one-eyed wino standing there. "Mr. Whitewall? Sorry to bother you, but my name is Mike, and I been a fan of yours for a long time now. I been real down and out, see, and lately I been real depressed. It's always been my dream to play you in chess. Whaddya say?" the man pleaded, sitting down and placing one of the cafe's chessboards on the table.

Jasper's ego had been rubbed, so he thought "Why not?" and they set up and started to play. Jasper played white, moved a knight out, and the circuits in his brain started activating. The smell changed from litterbox to a pine forest. Jasper inhaled deeply. Mike followed with his move, looking intensely at the board.

Jasper moved his other knight and the music switched to Mozart. He moved a pawn and flowers sprouted from the floor. When he moved the bishop, the walls began to fade. Mike foolishly left a rook open, which Jasper took immediately and the walls disappeared entirely, and he was in a field with rabbits hopping about.

"Good thing you're not wired," Jasper grinned. Mike was wincing and pointing his finger at possibilities. The way he held his face looked familiar. "You remind me of someone. Someone famous, Jimi Hendrix? Nah, it'll come to me."

Mike made his move, taking one of Jasper's knights. Clouds started forming overhead, and something was wrong with his coffee. Mike had made either a brilliant move or a very lucky one. There was a possibility of trading four or five pieces to his advantage. The counter rematerialized from Jasper's hallucinations. The blond kid was still back there.

"Are you sure this is decaf?" Jasper whined. The kid looked over at Jasper, glared, and turned away. The counter disappeared. It was Jasper's move, and he was forced into taking one of Mike's bishops, but it left him vulnerable. The flowers sprouted thorns. A rabbit bit him on the foot.

Mike never looked up in the next five moves as he traded pieces with Jasper. He lost the same amount of pieces as Jasper, but attacked his King's side and ended with good positioning.

Jasper's world was crumbling. He knew a way out of this, but the rain was falling heavily, and he couldn't concentrate with the rabbits chewing his feet, and the music was a wall of noise. All he could smell was sulfur. The chess pieces were incredibly hot, raindrops sizzling as they hit. His chair gave him splinters. He took a sip of his coffee and immediately spit the murky bile out.

"Aaaargh! Euyuck! What did you put in my drink?" Jasper yelled.

The blond-haired kid appeared suddenly, wearing a blood-splattered butcher's outfit with a huge knife in his right hand. "Look," he said, "if you can't keep all this yelling down, you're going to have to leave." With that, he faded away. Jasper heard snickering. He looked up into Mike's eye.

"What's the matter, Mr. Whitewall, something wrong?"

Suddenly, Mike looked just like Harvey Winchell. Jasper started to sweat. Even with the rain, he could feel his pores open up. He rubbed his eyes. This can't be Harvey Winchell, this must be a hallucination, he thought. Harvey's whereabouts are unknown, if this is him... Jasper knew he had to make the right move and fast. He couldn't concentrate good enough to remember the way out of this one, but there was always a way, wasn't there?

Jasper moved his remaining rook, which made the sulfur smell go away, but Mike countered by taking Jasper's queen. Stupid! Stupid! Stupid! Jasper thought, leaving her open like that! He stood up, the sulfur smell back and worse than before, and slammed his fists on the table. He looked down at his arms and saw maggots crawling from his skin. He felt the claws and teeth of evil rabbits crawling up his back, eating through to his spine. Harvey Winchell, it was Harvey Winchell! Only he could play like this, but it couldn't be him, but it was... Jasper tried to walk away, but the thorny vines grabbed his ankles and he fell. The rabbits jumped all over his face and started ripping away his cheeks.

"Yeeearighjiggh," Jasper yelled, rolling on the floor.

"Whoa, cowboy," the counterperson's voice boomed. "That's all for you. Saddle up and head back to the ranch."

Jasper managed his way to his feet and looked at Mike, or Harvey Winchell, or whoever it was. He pointed a leprous finger at him.

"I don't know how you managed this," he moaned, "but you'd..." Jasper stopped. Mike's other eye came back, his clothes were new, and he had well-groomed hair. He looked exactly like Harvey Winchell, and he was laughing the Winchell laugh.

"The only way you can stop this is to finish the game, and from your present condition, you should probably start playing a little bit better," his opponent warned.

Play? Play what? Jasper thought, I'm just a humble leper. I just want to find a dry place away from the wild animals. I want a little food in my stomach. Jasper watched a seven-foot red devil with cloven hooves and a pitchfork walk his way. "You'll have to leave now," it said, lowering the fork.

Jasper ran from the counterperson into the street. Extremely malicious furry animals, stuck in his clothing, bit him repeatedly. His right leg broke off and he tripped on it, falling to the ground. He looked up. The last thing he ever saw was a herd of chrome fire-breathing buffalo headed straight for him.

NEW SUIT, JUST LIKE MAYAKOVSKY
Gerald Williams

It was two o'clock in the afternoon,
and I was playing chess
with my sister's live-in boyfriend.
We were both out of work.
He'd been laid off by General Motors,
and was nearing the end
of his unemployment benefits.
I'd never possessed a real job—
at least not long enough
to get unemployment.
We were pretty broke.

"Is it my move?" I said.
"Yeah," he said, draining his beer.
We'd been playing chess all summer,
and I'd managed to win only one game.
Where his talent came from,
I'll never know.
He was a male stripper
before moving in with my sister.
I felt ill at ease around him.
He would always get rough
with me—wrestling holds
and quasi-martial arts stuff.
I'm not sure what he did at GM;
probably he worked on the line.

"Let's finish this game before
your sister gets home," he said.
And he was winning again.
I had a rook and a few pawns left.
He still had his queen, a knight,
both rooks, a bishop—
it was a slaughter.
I borrowed a beer from the fridge
and braced myself for the end.
He would never allow me to concede.
House rules.
He methodically captured all my pieces
and then immobilized my king.
It was the only decent thing in his life.

My sister eventually broke it off with him,
and he moved back in with his folks.
She didn't like the way
he treated her young daughter
and didn't much like him anymore either.
After a few days he returned,
wearing a brand new suit,
and asked if they could start over;
she stood her ground and told him no.
"Then I'm going to kill myself," he said,
and instructed her as to where
and didn't stop her from picking up
the telephone as he marched out.

The police found his body in the park
across from the station.
He had been a gymnast in high school,
so he stood between the parallel bars
and shot himself not once but *twice*
in the temple with a .32 caliber revolver.

That's determination.
To be wearing a new suit
in your final moments,
just like Mayakovsky,
without ever having heard of Mayakovsky,
though you are a laid off auto worker,
woman gone, no victories left in you at 26,
only half in this world now,
birds scattering,
the blue sky in knots above you.

UNEMPLOYED

I'M UNEMPLOYED AND I LIKE IT.

MAYBE IT'S CAUSE OF THE JOBS I'VE HAD. THEY WERE TERRIBLE BECAUSE THEY WERE JOBS.

I SPENT A YEAR ONCE AS AN ATTENDANT FOR A PARKING GARAGE IN NEW YORK CITY. IT WAS LIKE ALL PARKING GARAGES, I GUESS. LOTS OF CONCRETE AND 15-WATT BULBS. THE PLACE HAD A NAME. IT WAS CALLED "PARKING." IT WAS A SENSORY DEPRIVATION TANK; LIGHTS NEVER CHANGED, THE TEMPERATURE WAS CONSTANT. BUT WHEN SPRINGTIME CAME AROUND, I COULD TELL. THERE WAS A ROSE GROWING RIGHT OUTSIDE OF PARKING SPACE #206.

PARKING

5.00 ALL DAY UNTIL 7PM

A BRIGHT RED ROSE TWISTING ITS BODY THRU A JAGGED CONCRETE FISSURE.

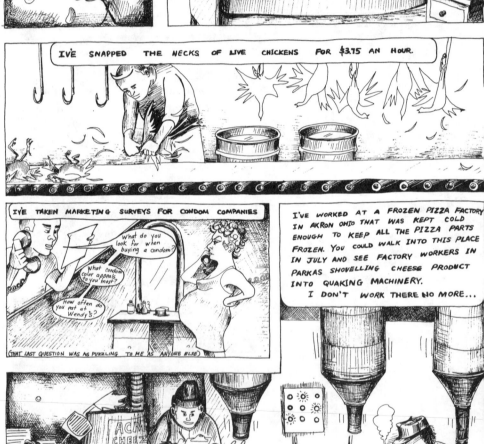

I'VE BEEN A GREASED WHEEL IN THE PERMANENT WAR ECONOMY MACHINE
Christien Gholson

I tested them, that's what I did.
Glass vials rolled down the chute
fresh hot from the spiderlike vial-making machine
and I tested them - the length, the width;
laid them delicate on a belt
rolling through a shotgun oven,
rattling down another chute,
waiting for me to leap from my stool,
stack them in crates,
run back to my seat,
test more vials.

I worked at the glassworks three weeks before I asked
the night foreman what the vials were for.
"Oh, they're detonators for Defense Department landmines."
The woman who sat across from me,
listening to Christian sermons-on-tape,
looked over at me
and smiled.

The click and scatter of the little vials
began their fiery chant for the rest of the night:
DEFENSE DEPARTMENT DETONATORS
FOR DEFENSE DEPARTMENT LANDMINES

DEFENSE DEPARTMENT DETONATORS
FOR DEFENSE DEPARTMENT LANDMINES

It came, high-pitched,
off hot glass,
molded perfect,
burning the fingers.

Legs, faces, and balls,
abstract as smooth hot glass
splintered and flew down the well of my hands.
I measured the length, the width.
In Nicaragua, El Salvador, Guatemala,
I measured the length, the width.
In Chile, Peru, Java, and Indonesia,
I measured the length, the width.
In Burma, Columbia, and forgotten deep Africa,
I measured the length, the width.
I measured the length and width of frightened skin,
of crying limbs.

I walked home,
jumping fences,
crossing snowfields,
steering clear of the streetlights.
Trying to outrun the store lights that signaled
        the new work day:

I saw bullets squeezed from icing cones in sunken-eyed bakeries;
trigger fingers grown in labs where students unwrapped fresh doughnuts;
armored cars sitting proud under dealership spotlights;
humming designs for the trajectory of cluster bombs
        crackling in the terminals of hungry insurance companies;
tank treads whistling dixie off conveyor belts in tractor factories;

shotguns forged by the careful taptap of cobblers in the back of shoe stores;
bayonets sharpened to perfection over the cutting boards of butcher shops;
the intercontinental ballistic missile's electric eye

      watching over everything from the center of each streetlight.
What was I going to do?

Two days later, the machine decided for me.
Contract fulfilled,
detonators finished,
new landmines created,
secret handshakes traded,
all extra workers were laid off.

Two men,
    on opposite sides of the world,
        crack a glass vial
          and disappear into the open mouth
                of a hungry dollar bill.

SLUMBER PARTY
Danielle Willis

Stacy was a trust fund brat from a wealthy family in Texas who worked with me at the Century and we made a lot of money doing rooms together because we both had long black hair and white skin and looked like sisters, but it was irritating sometimes because she was a junkie and any music other than This Mortal Coil or Chris Isaak grated on her nerves.

Between shows we'd go to Zim's so she could have pancakes with lots of syrup and vanilla ice cream, which were the only things she could stand to eat. She really wanted to introduce me to her boyfriend Ron because she said we looked alike, except that he was taller and had lots of tattoos. They were always fighting and finally Stacy put him on a plane back to Texas and set about trying to make me into a Ron substitute. This flattered my transvestite ego to no end but I'd never get high with her because at the time I was a major speedfreak and thought heroin was really boring. Heroin addicts are more romanticized but speedfreaks get so much more done.

At any rate, Stacy had something like fifty thousand dollars inheritance in the bank so she could afford a lot of heroin. Her condition deteriorated rapidly. One night in the Arena she was on her period and oblivious to the fact that her inner thighs were totally crusted with dried blood. I made her go wash herself but later she was finger-fucking me and her finger came out bloody. I freaked out and ran to the bathroom. It turned out I was having my period too and it was almost certainly my blood but I was so HIV paranoid and depressed I figured what the fuck and went back to her house and got high with her and sat around looking at pictures of Ron in black leather jeans playing guitar between bouts of vomiting. We really did look a lot alike.

Ron and Stacy made up a week later and she flew him back out to San Francisco, but pretty soon they were fighting again. One night at work after a particularly bad fight she kept trying to call him but there was no answer so she left work early to see if there was anything wrong. Half an hour later she called the dressing room, hysterical, begging me to come over because Ron had ODed on purpose and she was all alone in her apartment waiting for the coroners to show up. I got there just a few minutes after they left and Stacy was standing in the hallway clutching his black cowboy boots, which she had insisted on pulling off his feet before they took his body away. The house smelled of flatulence and sour milk and for a minute I thought her cat, which was lying unnaturally still on the cotton-littered sheets, had been ODed as well, but then it breathed and I didn't have to think of a way to tell her.

She told me she wasn't going to be able to get through the night unless she got high, so we took a cab over to her dealer's and copped eighty dollars' worth, all of which she shot into her ass as soon as we got back to the apartment. She had a theory that it was impossible to OD if you shot up in your ass.

After it hit her she stopped crying so much and led me into the bedroom and had me lie down on Ron's side of the bed and asked me if I knew how to raise the dead or at least talk to them. I told her no but that I'd put on some of Ron's clothes if she wanted me to. Stacy said that wouldn't be necessary because she could sort of see him hovering in the doorway and he seemed to be at peace. Then she nodded out and I tried on the clothes anyway but they were several sizes too big.

The next morning Stacy's mother came and took her back to Texas to clean up and a couple weeks later Stacy sent me a thank you note on floral stationery. Her handwriting was like that of a twelve-year-old girl sending a fan letter to someone in *Tiger Beat*.

GAZPACHO
Michelle Tea

1:30 a.m. gazpacho in my room
red and green and tasting
like tucson like too much
parsley and cocktails on
the porch, mezcal, tastes
like tequila someone played
a trick on we bought it cheap
in mexico two bottles per gringo
over the border gazpacho and
burritos enough to feed the
neighborhood and i did because
the neighborhood was crashing
at my house showing up at sunset
to eat at my cinderblock table but
it was cool i could afford it could
afford to pay rent buy groceries buy
jugs of red wine to get them all drunk
bongs of pot to keep them stoned and
gas tank full for road trips i
was making lots of cash and we were all
cool liberal fuck liberal we were
radical, anarchist cookbook beside
the moosewood cookbook on our bookshelf we
knew all about things like the

distribution of wealth and like i said i
was making tons of money and they weren't
making any they were unemployed because
finding work is hard or they're students or
in the emergency stage of the sexual abuse thing or
some other piece of laziness doctored up as
politics you know capitalism blah blah blah so
i was supporting an ever-changing band of lethargic
sunbathing potheads because i was making so much
money and yeah i was making it by leaving my body
so that strange men could fill it like a kind of
demon spirit but fuck it was my choice no gun
to my head no linda lovelace scene here and
i was really into communal living and we were all
such free spirits, crossing the country we were
nomads and artists and no one ever stopped
to think about how the one working class housemate
was whoring to support a gang of upper middle class
deadheads with trust fund safety nets and connecticut
childhoods, everyone was too busy processing their
isms to deal with non-issues like class
and besides,
you don't think rich families have problems
you don't think rich families have secret rapes and
alcoholic dads and feed their kids bad food with
sugar and preservatives i mean when you
get right down to it we're all just humans,
all on the same path to destruction because
our mother earth is being raped (is it ok
if we borrow that term from your
oppression, it's really powerful) anyway,
that class trip is just divide and conquer,

blood money is just a redundant phrase and all work
is prostitution, right? and it's so cool
how none of them have hang-ups about
sex work they're all real
open-minded real
revolutionary you know
the legal definition of pimp is
one who lives off the earnings of
a prostitute, one or five or
eight and i'd love to stay and
eat some of the stir fry i've been cooking
for y'all but i've got to go fuck
this guy so we can all get stoned and
go for smoothies tomorrow, save me
some rice, ok?

NOW WATCH HIM CRY
Shayno

It was so damn hot that night and my pain was killing me. I hurt, and the whole world was a distant planet. Me and my pain were all I could deal with. It was like I could only just observe the world around me, everyone and everything were so far outside my world of inner pain. Pain was my friend that night. I was going to see this band, just to check it out. So I get there and it's still hot and I'm still hurting inside like a howling dog. I'm just in so much pain inside that I can't talk to anyone, I'm in a shell of anger and, you know, pain. So the band goes on and I just can almost relate to this guy, the singer. But I can't relate, I can't relate to anyone, I never can. I can never get close, it's like my pain won't let me. I get a black coffee (which is the strongest drug I ever do) and I'm drinkin' black coffee and watching this guy flex his muscles and get all sweaty. He works out all the time, you can just tell and he's just there for me to watch. He's got all these tattoos and he looks hard and I think to myself, this guy has pain too, but not like me. My pain is insurmountable, my world revolves around my pain. So the noise goes on for about fifty minutes and then it's over and I'm drained and tired, but not too tired to get this man.

So I go backstage and he's there drinking water, and I ask him who he is. He tells me and I think 'I've heard of this guy,' he's got all these tattoos and he looks like a fucking jock. Like the jocks I used to hate in high school and I still hate now. This jock punk guy. He's all sweaty and wet and I get closer to him and I'm not feeling anything. It's just a reflex, there's nothing there but me and my pain. So he starts to get closer to me and I'm just staring at him and we're burning with need. He tells me about his pain but I feel nothing for him. He asks me to go to his room with him and I do and we just stare at each other because we have all this inner pain. Neither of us can connect, it's like that with me and all men, like I just go through the motions. There's nothing worse than having a man around, talking about men things and just bugging me and besides, I can't feel anything but my pain, man.

So I'm sitting there and he starts to take off his clothes and he's looking at me like a weak animal and he wants me, I know. His body is glossy with sweat and he's got this little hard-on going on and I know what he wants. More than that, I know what he needs. His skin glows white but black tattoos cover him and for a small moment I feel pity for him, it just slipped out, even though I never feel anything for anyone, it was like a blip of emotion. He lies on his back and he's looking up at me, begging me with his drippy eyes to take him in my arms and crush him. I touch his muscular arms and then I get on top of him and I'm just holding myself up against his naked, hard body. He asks me to take off my clothes and as I go to lift up my dress I backhand him in the face so hard that he is stunned. I clench my legs against him and I've got him pinned. All that weight lifting isn't gonna do shit for him now. He's struggling but I'm on top and he's fucked. I make a fist and slam him in the face again and again and his nose is bleeding and he looks confused, helpless. He is helpless, but I just laugh. I keep hitting him over and over until he is barely conscious and then I stand up over him and look him in his swollen eyes. He's moaning in pain and I tell him to shut the fuck up and I kick him in the jaw and blood is flying everywhere. I kick him again and then I step back and kick him in the balls, so hard that he bleeds and he's simpering and whining now, trying to curl up against my blows. I pound his chest with my fists and batter him pretty good all over and my pain, man, my pain is easing up. I feel great, like a junkie getting my fix. I roll him over and I kick him in the ass so hard he yelps. I'll search and destroy *you*, buddy. I step on him, over and over, stomping all over his broken ribs, I can hear them crack under my boot. Should I put him out of his misery? He's so damn pained but this pain is real, not that wussy inner pain no more, baby. His ass is black and blue and red so I roll him over and I bend over him and he's barely alive. I kiss his bleeding lips, his mouth is full of blood but I kiss him good and hard and he cries just a little. Right before he passes out, I say to him, "Nice story you wrote there, Henry. Real nice, ya shithead."

THE KNAVE OF HEARTS PROVES THE QUEEN OF HEARTS TRICKIER THAN IMAGINED
Justin Spring

This isn't one of your normal cases of repentance, one of your TV evangelists blubbering Oh Lord Jesus King and all of that. You know the bit: Do it, get caught, confess, do it again. This case is stickier. First of all, she never came into the kitchen unless I was there. So she could play on my weakness for metaphor. She'd deduced by the continuous articulation of my fingertips on the tabletop that the chambermaid was boring me with her passion for facts: the 11:32 out of Hartford stops at Coscob, Greenwich, three teaspoons to a tablespoon, you know the rest. She was right. I wanted the royal treatment in the worst way. We backed the Mercedes out of the barn, headed for town. For the bright lights. We were doing sixty when all of a sudden she was shoving me out the door like fast food. I hit the dirt running, slid into home head first. The back wheels were waiting. Somewhere there's a catalog on disk brakes I'd like to reference, just to make sure. Backed over me twice, said she didn't feel anything, just something pip-popping like chicken bones. Oh God, I can still taste the rubber, do it again.

SOME ARE POSSESSED
Dylan Halberg

Some are possessed of a darkness when love comes
across from the railroad yard, dodging the cars
as church bells spill mercy from their towers.
Some see spots and crouch before bad heart-valves
Children cry for mother and sleep in the piles
of clothes she left.   You come to me like
flowers in an alley, bringing me coins from shallow
wells, moving your teeth so beautifully I find
Insomnia wearing your love and kissing me in
even darkest rooms.   When the mailman comes
delivering autumn like an envelope full of dry
leaves, we will be there: perhaps holding hands
perhaps signing papers, but near if not enamored,
and surely that will redeem us to the clouds
that matter.

THE HOT DOG
Dan Buskirk

It was a real argument this time. Not a bicker, not a squabble, although even that would have been unusual. No, this time it was a root-of-the-problem, future-deciding type of argument, and I wasn't ready to deal. I walked the city blocks beside her in a sulking silence.

Finally, as diversionary tactic, I turned into a 7-11, walked up to the counter and ordered a couple of hot dogs from the polyester-smocked cashier. I looked at Cathy beside me, her quiet presence almost ghost-like, distant, un-there. When I met this woman two years ago, I felt instantly she would be an important person in my life. And she was. With her I was less alone. When I spoke she understood me and I, her. But after that other-worldly discovery faded, reality seeped in, and I was having trouble making the adjustment.

"That's a dollar twenty-nine," said the clerk, and I handed her a twenty. She looked at the twenty in her palm and held it back out. "I can't break this," she replied indignantly.

That was all the cash I had. My frustration built. The hot dogs were already in my hand. I turned and walked towards the door.

"Hey!" the clerk barked, but I barely heard her. I was already making plans in my head: Cathy and I would rob this 7-11 of two hot dogs, a modest start but just the beginning. We would hot-wire a car and be off through the Midwest, the scourge of the Southland Corporation. We would burst into 7-11s in town after town like Bonnie Parker and Clyde Barrow, liberating hot dogs, passing out free Slurpees to the working man as we held the grumpy clerks at gunpoint. Folk heroes on a crime spree, lovers on the run, police in heated pursuit as our Big Gulps sloshed around on the car floor beneath our feet.

"Put back those hot dogs!" she intoned louder to no avail. But the sound that stopped me in my tracks, a single step from the door, was Cathy's voice calling my name.

"Dan!" she called out scoldingly. She wasn't a step behind me. She stood still back at the counter.

I walked sheepishly to the clerk and handed over the hot dogs. She snatched them back in a huff. That clerk really needed a more graceful way to reject someone's twenty dollar bill.

Out on the street Cathy and I were arguing again. There's few things worse than being lectured on an empty stomach. "What's wrong with you?" she asked in a mixture of worry and disbelief. "You think you live in a movie or something. This is real life, this isn't a movie."

It could be, I thought to myself, if the cast would just stick to the script.

I WOULD KILL FOR NIGHTS FILLED WITH PAIN
Blacky Hix

It's hot tonight. All the windows are open. I am stripped to my underwear. I stunk of my own body odor today. Actually, it smelled pleasant. Summer is near. Summers are always painfully insane and joyous. I like isolation in the summer. Sweating in an empty room filling a notebook full of stories. Breathing in the doom, finding out what I am made of. Seeing how much pain and insanity I can put myself thru and still survive. I like to get in the demons' face and spit a little fire right back. That's my trip. If I am not in the process of destroying myself I do not feel alive. The rest of it becomes very fucking small and inconsequential in comparison.

I become possessed. I punch the walls. I scream. I do several hundred push-ups. The longer I last the more soul I earn. Yes. Alive in hell earning soul. My muscles tighten and burn. My teeth grind constantly. My hands ball into fists. I recite the mantra: fuck me, punish me, kick me, beat me, burn me, load me, cock me, kill me over and over again and again.

It is insane to live with a woman in the summer. I plot their demise inside the first week of June. It's a bad scene. She will say something like, "Two months ago you said you loved me. You don't even look at me anymore. I'm moving out. Do you hear me, Blacky? I'm moving out. It's over!" Even if I loved her I could not bring myself up from the bowels of hell to tell her. They leave. I keep burning, looking for my own end.

Summer: the Brutal God.

There are nights when I turn off the ghetto blaster and listen to the sirens. I think of the pigs responding to a call that a knife-wielding man is going thru a neighborhood knocking on doors at random and stabbing the unfortunate fucks who open their doors at 2:00 a.m. without asking who it is first. I think about some drunk running over a janitor as he is walking down the sidewalk to the 7-11 for a pack of Camel cigarettes. I see the drunk jump out of the car, reach into the back seat for the empties and the cooler with the twelve pack on ice. I see him run to the nearest house and chuck the shit over the backyard fence as the German shepherd barks madly, digging its claws into the wood. The drunk runs back to the car checking for any forgotten evidence. I hear the janitor moan. His head rests in a rapidly increasing pool of blood. Both legs appear to be broken in half, ribs crushed. Doors of houses open, people stand on porches pointing and talking. The drunk yells for someone to call an ambulance for Christ sake. The sirens die and fade with the distance.

I light a cigarette and contemplate a quicker suicide. I laugh at myself when I realize it's not the end I desire but the pain of the end. Death will come painlessly. Life will not.

GOOD ENOUGH AS IT WAS
Kimberly Strandberg

"We're sorry,
you see, we spend all
of our time
at the hospital
and haven't been
able to bring her
up properly."

He came home once
for a week before
he left for good.
He was sick, but I
was the problem
child.
He had a toy jeep
and G.I. Joe and I
wanted the jeep but
being five couldn't
explain that it wasn't
greed but I had a
surprise in store and
if I did explain
it wouldn't be
a surprise anymore.
I wished he didn't

have to cry but I
got the jeep
and ran to my room
where under my bed
I'd saved some
scraps of carpet
for the floor
of his jeep.
I returned
it quickly, but
his joy
didn't match
the grief of parting
with that jeep
in the first place.

CALIFORNIA
Aaron Cometbus

Heidi came to visit me at my place in Oakland. She sat at a little school desk and wrote stuff or drew. She ate peanut butter and marshmallow sandwiches and told me stories. I wanted Peet's coffee and some ice cream. "This place feels more like Arcata than Oakland," I said. "You're wider than you are tall," she said. "And there are shadows," I said.

Then I woke up. I was on a Greyhound bus passing through North Carolina. I shared my box of cookies with the old guy sitting next to me. He had a rad felt hat which I complimented him on. Then he fell asleep leaning against me and his hat fell off, revealing the huge bulging brain tumor the hat had been covering up. I didn't wake up because I was already awake. It wasn't a dream. I was on my way to Texas on the Greyhound. It was going to be a long trip. Since I couldn't wake up, I tried to fall asleep.

I made pancakes with Anna and Hollie late at night. I had to return to my junior high to make up a few missed high school credits. I had some amazing sex in the shower with someone I shouldn't have. I camped out on top of Grey's Bookstore on Solano with Jed. I went to a punk party at McCullum's ice cream parlor which turned into a huge brawl and Karen Zapata clocked Lisa Allbright over the head with a bottle.

Then I woke up. The bus pulled into Mobile, Alabama. Outside the station a boy bragged to me about fucking two dykes in a New Orleans hotel room after they'd picked him up hitchhiking earlier that day. I told him I'd had sex on Mars with two aliens who had picked me up while I was playing golf earlier that day. I figured it was a good trade, one lie for another. But he seemed angry so I got back on the bus. I tried to sleep.

Billie Joe was pissing me off. He took my goldfish out of the tank and was holding it over his head, pretending like he was going to eat it. So I punched him. Then he attacked me. Then I woke up. The Greyhound lights went on and everyone stumbled off the bus for a stopover in St. Charles, Louisiana. The driver pulled me aside and told me that I wouldn't be let on the bus in Houston unless I "changed my attire." It all seemed like a bad dream. But I wasn't asleep.

I snuck on the bus in Houston and got to Dallas where I met up with my friend Jess. Me and Jess headed west in his grandfather's camper. In El Paso I got way too sick and slept in the camper for twenty-six hours. I had horrible fever dreams about math and trying to figure out the same confusing situations over and over and over. Every time I figured anything out, I would wake up and write down the solution. But it was all in the dream. Then I would actually wake up, with nothing written down, and no solution.

I met Iggy Pop backstage at one of his shows. He was surprisingly nice and down to earth. Then I woke up. I was in Tucson. I was starting to feel better. We drove past Los Angeles and through the Central Valley, where Jess grew up. He told me about how some people there use tumbleweeds for Christmas trees, or boil them four times and eat them. I went to the back of the camper and fell asleep. I dreamed about getting home. Then I woke up.

ADAM
Lisa Taplin

Adam was a nice guy, the kind of person who would buy you a pack of cigarettes after bumming them off you the night before. He would sit quietly curled up in a corner of our couch reading the Marquis de Sade or his Horror Movie Bible while I emptied the ashtrays cluttered on the old leather trunk we used for an end table. When I got home from a class he would usually be watching MTV quietly, cracking his big white knuckles or filing his long transparent fingernails. He was polite to me, he knew he was an imposition and tried to make up for it. We made him pasta and couscous, instant potatoes and martinis so he knew he should be as inconspicuous as possible.

Adam knew my roommate would go off during the day with other men, but he didn't really mind since she let him sleep in her bed and fuck her when he needed to. I knew my roommate went into my room when I was at school and searched my pockets for money or things she could sell. Adam told me things when my roommate went to bed, about how she had dreams where I was trying to kill her or how she tried to dose my orange juice one morning, but the pitcher mysteriously fell over in the refrigerator during the night.

He cut my hair for free in the small yellow tiled kitchen, always starting long and asking me if I wanted it shorter. I liked that. His sharp nails felt good on my scalp. He was short and thin and very pale. This was because he started doing drugs when he was thirteen, he told me.

Adam was the kind of guy who had a lot of stories: how he got a stripper pregnant and ruined her career, how he got kicked out of this club for shooting up in the bathroom, how his sister wouldn't let him be alone with her kids. He was sad sometimes, but didn't ever burden us with his problems. When my roommate was with some other man, I would sleep in their bed with him. One time, he grabbed me violently in the middle of the night, sloshed around the waterbed, and pushed his dick against my butt, grabbing me from behind, his thin nails pressed into my breast. He was asleep and I lay very still. He loosened his grip and rolled over. I lay against him and wondered what my roommate did with him. She told me once that when she went down on him he could never come. He would jump up onto his knees and bang as hard as he could on the wall until he calmed down.

On my roommate's birthday I made a cake and decorated it with silver ball candies. He bought her some heroin and after he dumped it into a silver foil wrapper and tied it shut with a blue ribbon, we blew up the tiny smack balloons and scattered them around the cake which we put on the floor in front of the door so she would see it when she came home. Unfortunately, she wasn't feeling well and was in a bad mood. She ignored the cake and went straight for the silver package. I went for a swim and when I came back they climbed into bed with me and she told me about her visions and my flower print skirt and how I was a race car driver. Adam made her apologize, then they went into the living room to finish up her present.

Adam would go to the heroin-vending taco stand for her when she didn't want to deal with creeps. He would take the little smack-filled balloons in his mouth for her any day, and if the cops came he'd even swallow them for her, to fish out later. He'd buy a rig off a diabetic when she didn't want to deal with junkies. He won us tickets to concerts because he knew the answers to all the music trivia questions on the college radio stations. He tried to find my cat after she colored it pink with vegetable dye and he kept their fucked up friends from getting into my room when

I was trying to study. He went to the store for me. He didn't have any money so he paid us in other ways.

One time my roommate wanted Adam to cut her hair. When she went into the bathroom to shoot up I took the good scissors and hid them under the cushions in the couch. Adam saw me slide them under me and when she was searching everywhere for them, eyes pinned and convinced she was going insane because she swore she left them on the counter, he didn't say anything. When she began to cry because he had to use the shitty dull scissors, he just smiled at me over the top of her head.

Adam was forced to move out when one of my roommate's lovers died of a brain aneurysm. The last night he spent at our house we sat out on the concrete landing in front of our complex and smoked cigarettes as my roommate screamed and threw all of our glasses against the kitchen floor. Adam pressed my hand to his face and murmured his apologies into my trembling fingers. The next afternoon he packed up his books and his clothes and moved back to his parents' house, and I was left alone in that living room staring across at my roommate, jealous that Adam could escape so easily.

TO MY DAUGHTER ON HER
FOURTEENTH BIRTHDAY
Priscilla Sears

Just now, down in the root cellar, Sarah,
I found that bulb, fallen and forgotten on the dirt floor.
White shoots, tentative and thin, groped into the darkness.

I carried it up the stairs, cradling the dense head in my hand.
You put it in your forced fluorescent garden
Among the hyacinths, purpling
Precociously already, grown up abruptly.

I wish we could wait
Until some sure morning in May
When the springsweet ground has softened
Beside the warm stone foundation.

FATHER AND SON TALK
Darrin Johnson

You came to visit me
after getting out of rehab,
you put yourself there.
I was proud of that; showing signs you wanted to be sober.
You asked me if there was anything else I wanted to do with you.
"No," I replied. "I think we've done all of the touristy things we can."
You asked me again, looking me straight in the eyes. "Are you sure?"
"Yeah," I said.
not catching the real question until

I got that phone call from Mom
after you had flown home already
"This isn't a social call. Your dad is dead, suicide."
Then I caught it right in the face.

JUMPING THROUGH HOOPS
Mabel Maney

ONCE BITTEN, TWICE SHY

My grandmother spent the last five years of her life in bed, attended to by three Catholic nurses: Ruth, Violet and Lily.

She took to her bed the day after her little dog was bitten, not once but twice, by a big red dog.

HER MIND WAS MADE UP

Her mind was made up, there was no reason to leave her room. No one thought it odd; after all, hadn't her mother also retired young? After the first year, when it became clear she wasn't getting up, my mother and I moved in to take care of her, a job that mostly meant running to the drugstore for cold cream, cigarettes and movie magazines. I never saw her before noon. Neither my grandmother nor the dog was ever available without an appointment.

DREAMING OF YOU

My grandmother read every magazine we could find of interest to women; clipping articles and pictures and pasting them into scrapbooks. One of her favorite topics was The Kennedy Family And Their Tragedies. She liked Jackie Kennedy even more after the assassination, and kept a scrapbook just of pictures of Jackie in her blood-stained pink suit.

"Now that Jackie. She's a real lady," she liked to say as we looked at the book.

Now Pay Attention

My grandmother's favorite topic was Great Ladies And How They Lived. She was determined to turn me into one, having failed with my mother, who drank, often and in public. The summer I was ten she arranged for a series of daily instructional appointments, beginning at noon after her hair had been curled and her makeup done, and ending with the dog's walk at 4 p.m.

Today's topic is How To Pack One's Clothes In Such A Way As To Keep Them Looking Fresh And Wrinkle-Free.

"A woman must look her best and be prepared for the worst," my grandmother liked to say.

Jumping Through Hoops

Ruth, Violet and Lily were kept busy changing the linens and scouting out hairstyles for grandmother's weekly at-home beauty appointments with Mr. Jose of Mr. Jose's Coiffures. Of the three, grandmother liked Ruth best, and she became the only person she would see before noon.

On good days, Ruth, grandmother and I would mix a pitcher of grasshoppers and spend the afternoon drinking and playing gin rummy. On bad days I was sent to the library until Violet or Lily came to get me.

I was the best read person in my fifth-grade class.

Hat Of Fire
or
She Saw Luck Go Flying By In The Shape Of A Giant Martini Glass

That summer, Ruth became my best friend. We drank coffee at the kitchen table each morning, waiting for the signal that my grandmother had awakened, and dreading the time my mother would roll off the couch and make her way to the kitchen to rejoin the living, usually still drunk.

Lily, the youngest of the three and the most beautiful, moved to California, and a month later, Ruth left to join her. Mother said Ruth went for her health.

Grandmother shut her door and refused to speak to anyone, beginning a pout unparalleled in the history of my family.

Violet stayed on for years, but she never did learn how to play gin rummy, and, as my grandmother was fond of pointing out, had no head for hairstyles.

AS AMERICAN AS MOM, APPLE PIE and MARTINIS

by MARY FLEENER ©1991

YES, I COME FROM A FAMILY OF **"FUNCTIONING ALCOHOLICS"** THAT HAD DRINKING DOWN TO A **FINE ART!** BOTH MY BROTHER AND I GREW UP AROUND **LOTS O' BOOZE!**

WANT A BLAST? NEED A SMOKE?

EVERYTHING IN MODERATION!

MY GRANDPARENTS WERE THE ORIGINAL **PARTY PEOPLE!** THEY HAD A **BAR** IN A BEDROOM THAT HAD BEEN THERE SINCE THE **PROHIBITION** DAYS.

ACTUAL FAMILY PHOTO – CIRCA 1940'S

WE KIDS SPENT **MANY** WEEKENDS WITH THEM and MY GRANDPA MIXED DRINKS **CONTINUOUSLY.** BY AGE 8, I COULD IDENTIFY LIQUORS BY SMELL ALONE

GRAN'PA! ⸨SNIFF SNIFF⸩ YOU'RE MAKIN'...UH... ...DAIQUIRIS! ... RIGHT?

RIGHT!! ...WANT ONE?

YUCK! NO! THEY TASTE TERRIBLE!

UCLA

SHAKE SHAKE

HA! HA! HA!

I EVEN GOT MY **OWN NON-ALCOHOLIC COCKTAIL!**...A **"SHIRLEY TEMPLE"**..... (AND A **"ROY ROGERS"** FOR MY BROTHER)

...AND MY GRANDDAUGHTER WANTS A **BEER!** HA! HA! HA! NAWW... MAKE 'ER A **"SHIRLEY TEMPLE"**– BE SURE T' USE *MARASCHINO CHERRIES!*

WITH AN **EXTRA** CHERRY!

...VEDDY GOOD, MISS! heh, heh...

* TALK ABOUT CHEMICALS!!!

THEIR **SUNDAYS** BEGAN WITH **WHISKEY SOURS** IN BED. MY GRANDMA KEPT UP THIS HABIT UNTIL SHE **DIED!** (AGE 82)

SHIT! YOUR GRANDMOTHER CAN DRINK ANY OF US **UNDER THE TABLE!!** HOW DOES SHE **DO** IT?!!?

BYE! ⸨HIC⸩

YA GOT ME! I'M JUST GLAD YOU'RE DRIVIN'!

MY GRANDFATHER DIED AT AGE 63 OF A STROKE

MEANWHILE, MY **PARENTS** WERE HAVING **PARTIES** OF THEIR OWN. PEOPLE **STILL** TALK ABOUT THESE **"LUAUS"** IN THE SUBURBS OF **WEST COVINA, CALIF.!**

HA! HA HA HA HAHAHA

AND RANDY SAID
Fred Green

And Randy said
"Do you wanna do mushrooms?"
and suddenly   we were
walking & walking & talking & talking
for 12 straight hours
and Randy became afraid of the giant shadows
and he didn't want to go   this way
and he didn't want to go   that way
and I kept saying to myself
Fred   You're a good little Jewish boy
and you love your grandmother
and you love your grandfather

But then I heard the screaming

You're on LSD Fred   You're tripping
at a Grateful Dead concert   and I began
looking around at all the long-haired
veterans huddled-together so-serious
in their singing & touching of bongos and breasts
all—dancing so—wild through their hands—
and suddenly I was part of the very class
of peoples I used to despise in high school:
The Burnouts the Druggies the Heavy-Metal Kids
Who always sat at the back of the class...

And the streetlights held little baby rainbows:
I tried to calm Randy down

"Randy   lets pretend its a beer buzz"
we tried to talk about what we always
talked about: football Cindy Crawford Suicidal Tendencies 1st album
but then we started to question who we were
in relation to Suicidal Tendencies   and what was
our destiny in listening to Suicidal Tendencies concerning
all of this great and horrible   angry & dirty drug-filled
American world.

And there was hardly   anything to eat except
little burritos without the meat and i love meat
I need meat   because meat makes me feel   fat
and safe and stupid and ugly   and without meat
we were starving even more   alone.

And we finally met up with Ken and his girlfriend
Christine   She says "I've been up two days
Straight on acid and vitamin C tablets... I haven't
ate a thing... Sex Drugs Rock-n-roll.... Oh you guys did
mushrooms... that's great... they're so natural."

And suddenly sprinklers came on behind us looking like
giant wet spiders coming to get us when Ken
started running   then sprinting like a mad psychotic
and very white Carl Lewis and he was crying
that he lost control of his legs forever and
he began leaping like a giant bullfrog
and peeing all over his homemade tie-dye shorts.

And the ride home   was different
but   all the more the same   nobody mentioned
the stench flowing from Ken's shorts and Dave
began talking about football   like Dave always does
While me and Randy   just sat in the backseat
impatient   to get home   so we could go
and eat   McDonalds.

THE SECOND COMING
OR
FRED EDMONTON BLOWS A BIG ONE
Vampyre Mike Kassel

It was a beautiful September Tuesday afternoon in the olde history drenched hamlet of Cambridge, Massachusetts. The sky was blue, the air was as crisp as cider, and the maniacal motorists were happily engaged in wreaking merry mayhem upon each other in the convoluted mazeways that constitute the Cambridge street system.

I and my old friend and colleague, Peter Shean, saw none of it though, for we were deep within the smoky bowels of the Plough and Stars, Central Square's answer to the ancient question: What happens when you take a traditional Irish bar and relocate it on the border of the Twilight Zone?

We were knocking back pints of Guinness and listening to Jeff Beck and the Yardbirds psychedelically deconstructing Elmore James on the jukebox while some Irish emigre went from table to table trying to collect money to bail out some alleged IRA fugitive. At the next table, a bunch of MIT technerds were being harassed by a street psycho while, in the back of the room, somebody was jamming along with the Yardbirds on a mandolin. The jukebox switched to The Chieftains to Bo Diddley to *Danny Boy* as was its wont and, all in all, it seemed like a typical Tuesday afternoon in the Plough and Stars when Peter gripped my shoulders and turned me around on my stool, directing my attention to a somewhat seedy looking gentleman who had just entered the premises.

"Ya see that guy just come in?" he asked. I gave the guy the once-over. He was a short, pudgy, middle-aged character. He was wearing an old fedora, a houndstooth sport coat, and a pair of striped pants. His jowled mug put me in mind of an unappetizing mixture of Lou Costello and Richard Nixon.

"That guy is as full of shit as a Christmas turkey," Peter continued. "He'll spin you tales that Mother Goose would be ashamed to try and put over." Peter got off his barstool and started waving. "Hey, Fred! Fred Edmonton! Over here!" As the dumpy figure waddled his way over to us, Peter kept waving while muttering to me out of the corner of his mouth. "Check this out. This is gonna be good. His particular line of bullshit is that he's a big wheel, knows everybody. Last time I seen him, he tried to convince me that he knew the Pope from way back in World War II when he was in Poland fighting with the OSS. 'Everyone knows Fred Edmonton,' that's his big line. He's so full of— Fred! Good ta see ya! Pull up a pew. Lemme buy ya a drink. Fred, this is my old buddy Vampyre Mike. Mike, shake hands with the one, the only, Fred Edmonton."

Fred climbed onto the barstool next to me, settled his fat ass down, and thrust out a plump, pink, multi-ringed hand to shake. "Hiya hiya. Whaddaya ya hear? Whaddaya say? Shean, did I hear ya say you was buyin'? In that case, I'll have a pint of Guinness and a shot of Bushmill Black." He then gave me a searching look and said, "Don't I know you from somewhere? In Cuba with Hemingway?"

"Not me," I smiled.

"Princess Di's wedding?" he pressed me. "The Berlin Airlift? The last Madonna tour? Chappaquiddick?"

"I don't think so," I replied, draining my pint and signaling for a refill.

"Well, I know ya from somewhere. Your face is familiar. Hell, everybody knows Fred Edmonton."

The drinks came. Peter lit up a Winston, gave me a wink, and said, "So, Fred, what's up with you? I haven't seen ya in a month o' solstices."

Fred heaved a wheezy sigh, drained his Bushmill, and said, "Shean, you don't wanna know. I got nuthin' but hard luck stories. If I sold coffins, people would stop dyin'. If I sold lightbulbs, the sun would shine at night. I oughta become an arms merchant. We'd have world peace inside o' twenty minutes. My big problem is I don't seem to be able to stay away from show business. It'll be the death of me. It's like my good buddy Frank told me: 'Fred,' he says to me while we're hangin' around the pool with Dino and Sammy, 'Ya gotta stay away from show biz. It ain't nuthin' but a ruthless jungle and you're just too soft-hearted.' Jagger told me the same thing. So did Moe Howard. And Piaf. I shoulda listened to them but this deal was so big, I just couldn't walk away."

"What didja have cookin', Fred? Exclusive rights to produce the Second Coming?" Peter chaffed him.

"Pretty close, buddy boy, pretty close," he muttered while giving us a cagey look that reminded me of W. C. Fields peering pugnaciously over a poker hand. "I was only in the middle of producing the biggest musical comeback of all time."

"What were ya gonna do, Fred," Peter chortled, "bring back Elvis?"

"Elvis? Of course Elvis," Fred grumbled, "Biggest musical comeback of all time's gotta have Elvis but any putz coulda got ya Elvis. Brian Epstein coulda got ya Elvis. Bill Graham coulda got ya Elvis. But I got that other guy, too."

"What other guy?" I asked.

"That other bigshot singer who's supposed to be dead. '60s guy. Leather pants. Big lush. Likes to whip out his wazoo on stage."

"You mean you had a line on Jim Morrison?" I inquired incredulously. Peter just blew a smoke ring and rolled his eyes.

"That's the guy!" Fred barked happily. "Morrison! I was gonna make 'em a duet! Like the Righteous Brothers. 'You thought they was dead but Fred Edmonton brings 'em back alive!' "

"So what happened?" I asked, signaling the bartender to fill up Fred's glasses.

"What happened?" snorted Fred. "I'll tell ya what happened - I spend months negotiating with their people, tryin' to set up a meet. They're paranoid, see? Wanna make sure there's no *National Enquirer* photographers hidin' behind the curtain. Finally, I get the two of 'em and their people in the same restaurant. We're not there five minutes before they start arguing about billing. Elvis says he's gotta be top. Says he turned down the Kristofferson part in *A Star is Born* because Streisand wouldn't give him top billing. Morrison ain't goin' for it. Elvis says he should get top billing because he's the king of rock 'n roll while Morrison's just a Lizard King. I jump in with a compromise. 'What about co-billing?' I say, 'We could bill you as *A Pair of Kings*.' 'No good,' Elvis says. 'They'll think you mean B.B. and Albert.' Morrison ain't too thrilled with it either. Says he's plannin' to move back to L.A. and that a name like King could get him into some serious police trouble.

"Then Morrison pipes up and says he oughta get top billing because he writes his own material. 'Apart from being a singer,' he says, 'I am a poet.' 'I'm a poet, too,' Elvis announces. Says that since his retirement, he's taken to writing blank verse under the name of Cloudy. Says he's read at all the open mikes in Frisco and, once, even got Elmer Kaufdropp to give him a feature at the Suds and Duds laundro/bar. He proceeds to pull out a black notebook and clears his throat. Thank God the waiter intervenes at that point and says that if he hears any poetry being read, he'll 86 the lot of us.

"Morrison then gets on Elvis's case by tellin' him that he's hotter than Elvis now on accounta that movie that Oliver Stone made about him and Elvis allows that he's seen it and thought it was a pretty punk film. 'Oh yeah?' snarls Morrison, 'Well, *Clambake* wasn't exactly *Citizen Kane*, either. In fact, I'm a film school graduate and after checking out the rancid swill you put down on celluloid, I'd say that, if you're the king of anything, you're the king of the Elvis impersonators.'

"Well, that tears the rag off the bush. From then on, it's a yelling match over who had the biggest influence on rock'n'roll, who could fuck the most groupies, who had the better pout, who has the most professional impersonators, who had faked the most convincing death, who has the most disgusting weight problem, and who had the flakiest old lady.

Morrison blew the whole meeting to hell when he told Elvis that, while his old lady had lost all his poetry and ODed on junk, at least she didn't run off with his karate instructor.

"Well, at that, Elvis kicks back his chair and Morrison kicks back his and they're about to get into the porkbelly rock'n'roll grudge match of all time. I get up and jump between 'em. I get 'em calmed down. I get Morrison another half gallon of tequila and get Elvis another fried banana and percodan sandwich and, when everyone's mellowed out to an uneasy truce, I excuse myself and hit the little boy's room. When I get back they're both passed out at the table colder than a music lawyer's heart and stiffer than Warren Beatty's dick and their handlers are loadin' 'em onto hand-trucks and wheelin' em away and that's the end of a billion dollar deal, flushed down the urinal of fate."

He tossed off the last of his Bushmill and stared glumly into the depths of his Guinness. The jukebox finished up *Suspicious Minds* and started in on the Knickerbockers doing *Lies*. Peter just shook his head and gave me a 'what did I tell you?' grin. I clapped old Fred on the back and said, "Buck up, old man. Your day will come."

"I know it," he agreed. "I just know that this comeback racket is gonna be my ticket to easy street. This Elvis/Morrison deal was just a warm-up, just busy work until the real big deal gets sorted out."

"You got an even bigger deal on the burner?" I asked, astonished.

"Yeah," he answered, draining his Guinness. "It's in the works but it's gonna take time. I mean I got George, Paul, and Ringo all signed to play together again. Now all I gotta do is convince 'em that John's place should be taken over by JFK."

BULLSHIT IS AS COMMON AS MURDER
Sparrow 13 LaughingWand

Bullshit is as common as bibles; you can burn a ton and six more
will show up right behind you speaking in two-headed viper
tongues and you hear the tail buzzing way deep in the cancer
cowboy's chest telling you he's got your best interests at
heart.

Bullshit is as common as pennies and talk is cheaper than gumballs
these days   sweeter than lead and less fun than a rescue
mission in Sacramento where the common thieves and drunks
stand around talking

Bullshit while they munch on donuts blaming their whole sorry ass
trip on the devil and Agent Orange.

Bullshit is as common as herpes and when it tells you it loves you
there's disease on its breath hanging you up like your drunk
brother on the phone with some

Bullshit at two in the inescapable morning.

Bullshit is as common as lame poetry and more unavoidable than
those armed men who are there to protect you from

Bullshit like this is straight from the lab and god loves you and
the government doesn't want war and it's the best movie since
Repo Man and if i stopped drinking the world might end anyway
and breatharianism and immortality for anything besides

Bullshit that's as common as murder and jailhouse tattoos selling
bunk drugs in paint chip hotels where a cigarette burn on
the mattress tells you more about death than a splatter movie
festival.

God would give its eyeteeth to be as ubiquitous as
Bullshit because all the cigarette butts and bullets combined maybe
    add up to half the common
Bullshit that people keep dropping like pills and bastards until
    the world is up to its ass in
Bullshit and dying of it and it's really nobody's fault, not
    even the TV set or the President or the Guardian Angels but
Bullshit will be the death of us yet   crusted on the war cloud's
    bloody bottom gusting like ghost jiz out of diesel engines
    and tangling the air worse than barbed wire from every
    AM radio in every Gideon Bible fuckbox on the
    interstate where nobody's worried because
Bullshit kills you slow and easy while
Truth bites your head off like a geek and it's   over.

ROLLING INTO RED SQUARE
Bruce Isaacson

The Ugly American is British. He's filming for MTV a high concept film business fluke: a Harley Davidson tour of Russia. Mix it with a five-city Dave Mason tour and you've got MTV rockin' the hungry, Harleys rolling into Red Square, a comeback for a fading rock idol.

The Brit, friend of a friend of a friend, telephones from Riga. Needs, wants, please, hotel for him and the crew when they pull into St. Petersburg about 2:00 a.m. He wants it guaranteed and gives me his American Express card number. That's about as useful to me as plutonium in ancient Egypt, but it seems like an expression of sincere desperation. We pay for the room then he doesn't show up. Telephones the next morning: don't worry, he'll pay, let's meet at noon. At noon he calls, let's meet at three. At three he calls, let's meet at nine. At nine, let's make it ten-thirty. At eleven, I'm waiting in his hotel, he's not there. Go to phone the room, and there he is in the lobby.

Now I get to hear his story about the tour. They've got twenty-five Harley Davidsons and seven stretch limos for the crew. Only half of the Harleys got shipped. Two more broke down when they got here. Do I know where to get parts for a Harley in Russia?

Me, I'd just like to get a good bath. At Olga's mother's two-room apartment, the five of us are in the middle of twenty days of no hot water. But sitting with the director in the hotel brasserie, I begin to see the real story. Now, the director's translator is arranging twenty percent of the hotel bill for himself. Now, the man who's supposed to feed the crew is keeping the money for himself. Now, the Russian camera crews appear, hollering that they're going hungry.

Now, even the American who arranged the hotel is angling for a cut. This director's got a Soviet fortune, and we have the savoir-faire of crows over carrion. And here I am making it all possible, helping to liberate foreign dollars for Mama Rus. What the hell, I'm right. I'm over here eating cabbage, squatting on a slit wound in the earth. All of this is unavoidable. It's the steam train of centuries of need, sliding into the oil slick of all the greased palms of Hollywood.

Now I am the Ugly American, going native, arm-pitted winner of the cold war, listening to the director's bad stories just so I can eat in the hotel restaurant. The director, with his double soft voice, tiny frame, and pockmarked druggie intonations, saying how this whole shoot has been crazy, but he thinks he's handling it all pretty well. Everyone else is yelling, Dave Mason is threatening to cancel the last three shows, *I've gotten to know him really well, I mean frankly he can be an incredible asshole, but we're really close, I mean, we've cried together.*

I want to tell you this in confidence, he says, leaning in, *but things aren't what they seem. The big director in the main shoot in Moscow? He's never made a movie before. Everyone's crazed, that's why I've been crying so much on this trip.*

And those guys on the Harleys aren't really bikers. One of them's a doctor, another one's a lawyer, and one is president of an electronics firm in the Valley. They each paid $8,000 to ride Harleys in Russia, but now they're acting like biker trash. I mean, they're fucking anything that moves. I don't understand these Russian girls. I mean, a hundred roubles and they're giving blowjobs in the lift. They're all acting crazy, why do they fuck so fast?

I interrupt him long enough to say I've never once been approached by a Russian prostitute. My wife is talking intensely with one of the Russian cameramen about these $70,000 movie cameras they're carrying. But the director's back at his monologue.

At our Moscow hotel the prostitutes phone all night long, then sometimes they just drop by. And these corporate biker guys are doing the whole tour. I think I'm handling it all pretty well, but I sure would like to get some pot, do you know where I can get some pot?

I just miss my wife, would you like to see a picture of my wife? He shows a photo of an attractive Japanese woman all around the table, pushing it at the Russian camera crew, who don't have any idea what this means. Then back to his monologue in English.

My wife and I, we speak Japanese, actually. The only one I can speak Japanese to on this trip is the guy who's financing the movie. He's this incredible Japanese guy, I mean, we've cried together. This whole mess is gonna cost him at least a million dollars, and I'm worried about him. He's going to be in horrible emotional shape when this is over.

Olga and I finally get out of there with the money he owes us plus taxi fare to boot. Once he got his wallet open, the guy's handing Franklins around like Kleenex. The next day he's on the phone to us. Wants us on staff to arrange locations. He doesn't trust his translator. Thinks the translator's holding out on him, taking money for himself and fucking up his instructions to the crew.

I can tell the director's in the grips of paranoia—that special feeling that comes over foreigners when they realize everyone's been playing them like a slot machine. Also, in this case, there's some kind of narcotic deprivation thing that gives his accusations a hollow tinny sound, like someone who thinks he's living in a *Thin Man* movie but is behaving more like Bette Davis on a rampage.

But those hundred dollar bills are still mouthing platitudes in our pockets, and we agree to come to the hotel. First thing, he starts back in handing out Franklins. Now I'm translating for the director. From his instructions in English, I translate for Olga into Spanish, and she gives his instructions to the crew in Russian.

It's all happening in the Czar's Palace Hotel, downtown St. Petersburg: five star, diamond chandelier, gourmet room service, fountains, Michelangelo reproduction sculpture. When there's a lull, opening a notebook to write this... So that today, if film people are maybe the closest thing to some sort of royalty, that makes me the court poet, scribbling it all down. This is history, the way the Russian who'd been pocketing the food money looked like a crestfallen five-year-old boy when the director sent him packing back to Moscow.

And the director, with his uncombed shoulder-length hair, blabbering some bullshit line to get filming rights from the Kirov Ballet. And the bodyguard, retired black beret, evaluating us as a threat to security. And me, angling to get an hour alone in the hotel room just to get underneath the five star shower.

At the end of the first day's shooting, there's news. In Kiev, Dave Mason's thrown a fit over concert facilities, called off the concerts, and gone home. In Moscow, a motorcycle accident. One middle-class biker dude dead. Two more in critical condition. The American crew is going home. The Russian cameraman tells us it's a prophecy. Anyone who can get out of here, he says, should.

RITES OF SPRING
Ann Chernow

In the meadow,
sunglasses and double-breasted
suits mingled with bare feet and
wildflowered dresses.
Sheep were grazing guests
rubbing against herringbone
and homespun.
Betsy and Bob were married
by his father's rabbi
and her mother's lover,
a lesbian priest.
After the "I do's"
cows mooed, goats bleated,
granola was tossed
instead of rice.
Someone said,
"If you're born a cricket
you die singing."

NOTHING TO LOSE
Riba Meryl

Sick and tired she says to the guy
sick and tired of all the stress
and the mess
and the
puff puff
clouds of smoke
billowing upwards
random strokes of good fortune
all too few she says
all too few
and he says
foam mustache
belching satisfaction
another audible gulp
of cold refreshing swill
wipes his mouth with his hand
I know what you mean
it's enough to
coughs his brains out
for ten minutes straight
nasty revolting painful sound
lights up another cig
drive a person crazy
what with all we have to do
spits into a napkin
just to survive
she nods in agreement
totally nauseated and says

what does a person
have to do
what does a person
have to
pulls the last few dollars
out of her wallet
damn thought he would
offer to pay
do
to make ends meet
to make love sweet
to make world peace
to clean up the streets
to believe in your dreams
to grab something to eat
to get enough sleep
I don't know
I just don't know
oh let me get this he says
manly take-charge hand gesture
accompanying wallet withdrawal
from name-embroidered garage shirt
pocket

guesses it was worth
enduring this neanderthal
after all and
puts her money away
thanks she says
it's nice to know
someone understands what I'm
maybe ask her out for dinner
going through
she can always use a good
free meal
say what are you doing

Friday night
he asks
well nice enough she supposes
might as well
nothing
wha'dya have in mind
nothing
how 'bout dinner
nothing
sounds great
nothing to lose
anymore

SWEET C
Marci Blackman

I was standin in the kitchen when Mama told me. Leanin against the refrigerator. Head down. That's how I always stood when I didn't know what to say. The linoleum was goin soft, bubblin all over the place. Kinda like Mama these days, only the linoleum wasn't brown. Kinda yellowish was more like it.

I remember it cause Mama was boilin greens, and at the same time the pork smell started fillin my nose, that old shit started fillin my head again. *Nine years.* I hate it when that old shit start rushin in like it ain't got no place left to go after it done been round the world and back. *Nine years.* Like some spoiled little brat you was glad to get rid of, run away. Then, after nine years, decided the Man's world wasn't such a place after all. Come back to haunt you like you ain't never been haunted before.

Don't know what she thought I was gonna say. Maybe she was tryin to see where I was at. "I hear Miss C's comin home t'day," she say, drawin it out slow-like, tryin to see if my face was gonna change. I didn't let on, though. Just stared at that ol sorry linoleum a while longer, then made like I had to go someplace.

"I heard," I say. "I got to go."

"Got to go where?"

"Out."

"What about Tyisha?"

"What?"

"You got somethin goin on?"

"I might."

"Oh, ol girl, you ain't got nothin."

"I got to go. I ain't gonna be but a minute."

"I'll tell you what, child, you better learn to slow yoself down. Ain't gonna be long fore that child start screamin fo her motha. Pretty soon, you ain't gonna have no choice."

"Bye."

"You best be thankful yo mama didn't do you like that. And..."

I could still hear her after I done closed the door and started down the hall. I tell you, that ol girl got some lungs on her. But you know, I didn't really have no place to go. I just said that. I knew C was supposed to be gettin out about now, but, you know, somehow I let myself forget that it was today.

Nine years. I guessed I'd go on over to the park. That's where I'd usually go when I didn't know where else to. Just hang out-like. That's mostly what I do now, hang out... and go pick up my check twice a month. Don't smoke no more now. Not really anyway. Though seems like everybody be doin it now. When C and me used to hang out, didn't seem like there was so many. And all the shit that's out there now, you lucky if you know what you got. Niggas be tryin to sell anything nowdays: soap, bakin powder (if they can afford it), hell, ha, ha! They even be tryin to come up off some wax and act like they givin you a good deal. You know, sometimes I think if we spent half the time bangin the Man the way we do our own selves... But, then, I guess it don't make no difference. No matter what we do He gonna figure out some way to keep us down. Sure don't help none us keepin our own selves down, though.

Me and C never got bad shit. Mostly on accounta C. Cause that girl used to know how to work *everybody*! She wasn't no strawberry. Didn't have to be. And we paid most everytime. Sometimes we got credit, cause they always knew C was good for it. And the way she walked. It was sorta like she was movin in slow motion. Almost like she had got some the night before and was still feelin it. And, every time she passed by, the boys would start rubbin on they thing, and droolin all over theyselves. And that's why we never got no bad shit. C made all them niggas feel like she belonged to each one of em. Every once in a while though, she'd give it up to one, kinda like in good faith. But it didn't mean nothin to her. "Strictly business, baby," she'd say. Sometimes when wasn't nobody lookin, I'd try walk like that in the mirror. One time C walked in on me and started laughin. At first, I was too through. She just kept laughin and laughin. "Girl," she say to me. "You got to have a whole lot more than your eighteen years fore you can walk like Sweet C. That's my trademark, girl." Then she showed what I looked like in the mirror, and we both started laughin. "Why you think peoples always so good to me?" she'd say.

"Cause of the way you walk?"

"Cause I'm sweet, girl. Sweet and smooth like chocolate."

You know, I can't remember not one day I made it from the house to the park without somebody fallin in step with me. This time it was Big D. Big D was one of them niggas thought he had to watch my back, and help himself to my snack after C went up. I didn't mind it so much. Least D was cute. It was all them other ones who thought the same way that worked my nerves. Act like they own you, take what they want when they want it. Then when the baby start cryin, ain't not one of em around to say they the one who made the baby cry. At least D still act like he cared some, even if he did say Tyisha wasn't his. And even if she was, wasn't no way I could be sure cause all them other niggas. But he did always ask about her. "How's that cute little girl?" he'd say.

"Lookin just like her daddy," I'd say. Then we'd both start laughin. You could always tell when Big D was about to get serious. He'd get real quiet-like, and look down at his feet, like he was tryin to see if he was walkin straight or somethin.

"Goin up to the park?" he'd say. I'd just kinda nod my head, cause I knew he was gettin serious. "You been hangin a lot lately, ain't ya?" I just kept noddin. When D got serious, it was best to just let him speak.

"Don't be smokin up that baby's check now, girl."

Now, it was time to say somethin. See, D mighta meant well and all, but we both knew he was gonna keep stride with me right up to the park, and sit beside me till we was finished smokin to our heads - no more money left between us. Then he'd go on and fall in step with some other ho.

"I ain't smokin up nobody's check. Is they some reason you so concerned about *my* baby?"

"Hey, I'm just lookin out for you, that's all. And if you ain't gonna look after yourself, least you can look after your little girl."

"Well, thank you kindly, but I'm lookin out for me and mine just fine."

He got silent for a while, then tried to change the subject. "You hear?"

"Hear what?"

"C get out today."

"Yeah, Mama told me."

"You talk to her?"

"Nope."

"You see her at all?"

"Nope."

"She know about Tyisha?"

"Nope."

"Bet you glad she comin home, though?" This time, I just nodded my head.

Truth was that most of me was real excited C was gettin out; that things was gonna be like before. But part of me was scared. C used to tell me I just had nervous stomach. She was all the time tellin me that. Sometimes I wondered why she let me run with her. I wasn't but eighteen that first day I saw her over to Ronnie's. She musta been thirty, at least. I couldn't help starin at her. And the way Ronnie and the rest of the fellas looked like they just wanted to gobble her all up, but at the same time was afraid to. I just kept starin and starin, mouth fallin open and everything.

At that moment, I didn't want to be like her, I wanted to *be* her. She had all the say so — the last word in everything. You knew it, too. Just by lookin at her. And she knew you knew it, just by lookin at you. She used to tell me she saw herself in me. How she was before she got so wise. She said sometimes she missed that girl and that was why she liked to keep me around; to remind her of her.

C was always real good to me. It was like I was her younger sister or somethin. She was always gettin me out of some trouble I had backed myself into. I remember the first time I hit the pipe, and I told her about it. I was so scared. I thought she was gonna go upside my head. But that's when she got me smokin Mo's Primo's. She said the high lasted longer, and that the combination of the weed and the rock kinda canceled each other out.

"You don't never heara no people dyin from a heart attack after they smoked a Mo," she'd say. Truth is, I like smokin Mo's better than hittin the pipe. Seem like on the pipe you got sprung faster. And you was always tryin to get that first buzz back. That buzz that went straight to your head after you hadn't had none for twenty-four hours or so. The one that sorta hung out with your brain cells, ticklin em like. You be sittin on the floor, with your back against the bed, and after that first hit your head would sorta tingle and you just let it roll back. *Cush*. It would hit the bed so soft. And for a minute you was just... gone. Then you spend the rest of the night tryin to find the place you went to. Fore you knew it, you was on your hands and knees, tryin to smoke any little white yellowish piece of somethin you could find. Mo's wasn't like that. With Mo's, it hit you gradual-like. Then, you came down easy, ate a little somethin, and went to sleep...

Yeah, C took care of me. Mama didn't want me to have no parts of her, though. Mama don't never cuss. God and the Devil do just fine for her.

"You out there runnin with the Devil," she'd say. "Playin in hell's fire. What in God's name do she want wit you anyhow? She old enough to be yo motha."

"Mama, please!"

"Well, you never know in this day and age, the way y'all be spittin out babies."

"C ain't the Devil. You just don't know... Least I got somebody to look out for me."

"You two funny?" I just looked at her, stupid-like. "Yeah, well, you go on. You hear? Go on. Cause God gonna take the Devil down. And, baby, anybody who be wit him gonna go too."

I think, maybe, after Tyisha come along, Mama wished I still had C to look after me. Even if we was *funny*. Though, sometimes I used to wonder if C wasn't. The way she used to look at me. Sometimes she used to touch me too. Real soft-like. She used to run her fingers up and down the back of my neck; tell me never to be scared of nothin. "Don't be like me," she used to say. "Don't let nobody tell you can't do nothin just cause you black and female." I didn't know what she was talkin bout. Nobody never told me I couldn't do nothin. Come to think of it, they never told me I could, neither. It felt real good when she touched me, though. Made me relax, feel safe. One day she told me she loved me, and if anybody ever fucked with me she'd kill em. Showed me the gun she'd do it with, too.

I guess I did love C back then. Now'n I ain't so sure. Truth is, C kinda scared me. Made me feel things I didn't wanna feel. Love is some serious shit. You know? I know I didn't love Big D, or whoever it was made my baby cry. But C protected me. I never wanted to be, or be with someone as much as C. Yeah, I think maybe I did love her. But then I hated her. Hated that she left me out there with all them niggas before tellin me what to do with em.

She fucked up. What in the hell was she doin lettin some white ho she ain't never seen before come into her hood, and buy some shit off her. Kinda make me think she wanted to get caught. Wanted to leave me alone out there with all them niggas and they shit. She knew I was sprung.

What the fuck was I s'pose to do?

I did go to see her once. Ain't been back since. It was right after she got popped, before she went up. Even still she didn't tell me what to expect. She was laughin and jokin. "Don't worry, baby," she told me. "Got me a lawyer. Gonna be out Wednesday." She looked good, too, even in jail clothes. I told her, maybe I get sent up too. Looked like fun. She say don't even joke about it. I say, 'Ey, it'll only be till Wednesday. Still, she say don't joke about it. Told me she'd call me, tell me when to come to the station to meet her. Ain't seen her since. 'Ey, and you know what the bitch about it was? Mama the one who told me they sent her up. Shoulda seen the look on her face. All pleased with herself and shit.

Still, wasn't nothin like the look she got when I told her I missed my time. You know, it.... different. Most people think when they tell they mama somethin like that, she gonna wanna kill em and bury em right there on the spot. I remember Mama's eyes kinda burned through me, hot-like. Went straight through my eyes to the back of my head, crawled down my throat, through my lungs, wrapped theyselves around my heart and squeezed me till I started cryin. She musta tried to squeeze both her pain and my pain right on out. I remember it cause she was bastin a bird. Seemed like Mama was always cookin somethin. The bastin brush froze, then dropped to the floor, practically standin up on that ol sorry linoleum. Then, she hollered as if she was gonna bring the house down. "Oh, my Lord Jesus, God Almighty! Tell me what to do with this child, cause I done grown tired."

What surprised me was that it was the first time I missed my time. First time in damn near nine years. And, four years before that! Plus, the way I saw it, and still see it I guess, is that twenty-eight years old ain't exactly no child. Yeah, a lotta years done passed since C went up. A lotta shit done gone down. Now I'm keepin step with Big D to the park, and C gettin ready to come home. I guess what scares me is that she gonna expect things to start up from when she left, and truth is, I kinda want em to. Cause seems like after C went up, I stopped learnin. But you know, a lotta things can happen to people in nine years. She don't even know about Tyisha. What she gonna think? What she gonna say when I tell her how I shared my blood and my food with some... some thing that made me throw up, livin inside me? How she gonna act when I tell her how much it hurt — all them niggas goin in and outta me? How it hurt deep down in my heart-like; made me want to call out her name and ask where the hell she was! How I cried when they held my shit just out my reach till I spread my legs.

Then what she gonna say when I tell her how my belly grew? How I started to kinda like it. How it was so smooth and brown. How it felt the first time little Tyisha kicked. How they put this thing on my belly and tried to tell me whether my little baby was gonna be a boy or a girl. And how I wouldn't let em. And how I loved that little thing inside me. And how they took it away.

Yeah, that's right, C. They took my baby away, cause I was sprung, and so was she. Wouldn't even let me see her; tell her I was gettin myself fixed up, so I could come and take her home. It hurt C. It hurt real bad. First I had this life growin inside me, then they took it away before I even got to see what it looked like. And the only way I could find out was to give up the one thing that got me through these last *nine years*. But I did it, even if it was only for a little while. I brought my baby home. Oh, C, she was so beautiful. Didn't look like me at all. All I wanted to do was look at her.

But then she started cryin. Cryin and cryin. I couldn't take it. I wanted to backhand those tears right off her face. Finally, I just didn't care no more. She'd scream, then I'd scream back. She'd scream, I'd scream louder. I didn't know what to do, C — how to shut her up. One day, she was cryin so hard, I thought her lungs was gonna come up through her throat. Then Mama picked her up and rocked her real gentle-like. You shoulda seen her, C. She just up and stopped cryin. I remember I was shakin like... I don't know what. I couldn't breathe. I had to go. Next thing I know, I was fallin in step with some nigga, on my way to the park.

Nine years. I noticed Big D was starin at his feet again. Swear, I ain't never seen a nigga stare so much at his feet. Now what was he gonna say? Ain't neither one of us said nothin for the longest time. You'd think he'd just wanna keep quiet till we got our shit. Uh oh! Here it come. Nigga done looked up. Then the strangest thing happened. I ain't never seen so many things go through a nigga's eyes. Happiness, fear, excitement, sadness. They was all there. Trip about it was, he wasn't even lookin at me.

When I turned around I saw this skinny old woman hobblin towards us. Now what she want? We ain't even got our shit yet. I looked at Big D but he was still standin there; all that shit still goin on in his eyes. As she got closer, I don't why but I felt my knees go to shakin. She wasn't no bum or nothin. That was sure. Her clothes was too nice. All of a sudden-like, I heard D speak. "What up, C? Long time." I think my mouth about dropped down to my feet. We looked at each other, hard.

She said, "What up?" and hugged me. I didn't say nothin. Couldn't. Just nodded my head, and tried to smile. I looked deep-like into her eyes, saw my reflection. Almost started cryin.

"I got to go," I say. "Mama's watchin Tyisha. Come by the house sometime, C." She said she would.

I went home and grabbed Tyisha out the crib. Started rockin her like I'd seen Mama do. I knew Mama was watchin me. "You see her?" she say.

"Nope."

You know what's funny? Ain't nobody ever keep step with you when you leavin the park.

CHOCOLATE CRAVING
Lynda S. Silva

mama always did say
i'd come to a bad end
'cuz i loved brown sugar
craved chocolate

and, oh lordy, his walk
half going ahead
the other half
catching it up and
passing it
just about lays me out

...picture my body cloven
spread with thighs
moisture between them
like a crushed grape
as i feed on him
turning his tongue
stickily in my mouth
like a greedy bite
of old-time malt taffy....

but it ain't gonna happen
not here, baby, not
in this neighborhood
where every corner
knows your name
and every mother's broom
sweeps the stoop
with an eye for
them don't-belongs

mama's right i guess
that damn boy leaves behind
black, blowby want
like a fly leaves
infectious germs
and i still got
the cravin

GRIEF
Carole Vincent

For a while, she says
the alcohol works.
Then less.
Finally it ceases altogether.

He hands her the round
slice of ham
out of his egg McMuffin.

She stares at it dully
in nonresponse.

She knows she can't keep
this up.
He cries whenever she mentions
his wife.

She'd like to try
getting stoned
but he won't let her.

He tosses his underwear
on top of the candle.
Smoky vanilla, a fire
fills the room.

She puts his erection on hold
as she answers the phone.

He understands.
She is expecting an announcement
of death.

ANNUAL VISIT
Buzz Callaway

Thanksgiving was coming up and Jane wanted to go home to see her mother. Normally I would have gone with her, cause I like her mother and I like Detroit but we couldn't afford for both of us to fly. That was too bad. It's important to get out of the city sometimes. And Detroit is just the place to go. Motown is at the cutting edge of urban America. In the '70s, when the country's cities seemed to be charging headlong for a cliff, I thought New York was leading the pack. But there was Detroit, a little puff of dust at the bottom.

Jane's mother looked just like her, only pasty and bloated. She had the upturned nose and blue, almond eyes, the blond hair and laser lips. She lived by Tiger Stadium on a little street off of Michigan Avenue. Connected two family clapboard houses lined the street with shops on the corners. She had two rooms which she rented from a woman named J.D., in a house by a vacant lot full of weeds and stray dogs. She fed the dogs and picked the wild flowers, some of which were very beautiful, especially these button-like yellow ones which turned into globes of white dust when blown. I could have called her Norma, Jane did, but I liked to call her Mrs. Esposito or Mrs. E, out of respect.

I never met Mr. Esposito but I've seen his picture on Mrs. E's mantle piece. This is where I always turned to first upon entering her apartment. There were pictures of Jane as a baby and child, plump and smiling, biting her tongue. In a white party dress with braces and freckles. As a freshman, in a plaid Catholic girl's uniform, white button-down shirt and full pubescent breasts filling out the jacket. Then her graduation picture, cap and gown, long curly blond hair and round gold wire glasses. These were in ornate brass frames with crimson velvet backing, and plexiglas cubes. Then there was one of her mother and father standing by a row of cottages by a lake, smiling and young. Her father has a crewcut and is clean shaved. Another of him in the army, big hat and spiffy uniform. Then one of the whole family in front of a tiny house with plastic flowers. He is heavier, with a full mustache. Jane looks to be about twelve, in cut off shorts and a halter top. Her mother's in black spandex and a tube shirt. No one is smiling.

In the early pictures Mr. Esposito looks straight and serious. They are in love. His eyes are black and deep. By the end he looks sick and tired. The eyes have sunk into rings. From what Jane and her mother say he was a great guy. Mrs. Esposito was eighteen when she was pregnant with Jane. The father ran off and Mr. Esposito, just back from Vietnam, was in love with her and they got married. Anyway, six or seven years ago, he got killed by a robot at the Ford plant. Mrs. Esposito left the suburbs and moved back to her old neighborhood.

J.D. took care of her. She lived upstairs. The downstairs was divided into two apartments. Mrs. Esposito occupied the back one, which looked out on a fence and little concrete yard. Mr. Durell lived in the front. You never heard him but every morning and night he would take his dachshund for a walk. He was always dressed in striped pajamas and running shoes. He smiled and nodded his fat head at us but never said a word, reserving all conversation for the shivering, high-strung monster at the end of the leash.

If J.D. didn't play cards and talk to Mrs. E and occasionally feed her, I don't know what would've happened to her. After Mr. Esposito was killed she went into a deep alcoholic depression. J.D. sensed her grief when she came to rent the place and gave her the apartment cheap. She asked her up to watch TV. She told her not to drink too much. But most of all she made her laugh. They fought like sisters.

She had bought the house with money she got hitting the numbers. I don't quite understand how she ended up in Detroit. She was born in

South Carolina. Her parents were migrant farm workers, but she hated farm and factory work and got a job in a restaurant. Eventually she came to New York, and opened a restaurant in Harlem. According to her, she had lost and gained a score of businesses, including a private gambling joint, worked as a housekeeper but mainly kept moving, making money. She had a son whom her mother raised, but went on to bring up three kids who were not her own. When the last went to college, she wanted to move on and just came to Detroit. Something was missing, probably a man, but she never included it in all her rambling reminiscences, which were charming and filled with broadly comic impersonations. She could do a group of junkies walking down the street, all of them, or a preacher, a con man, a lazy worker, an old man, whatever. And her food was amazing. When she cooked the whole block could smell it.

Going out to Detroit in the summer was especially good. The houses had connecting backyards and porches. It was an integrated neighborhood, Black, Mexican, Polish, Italian, and Irish. During the day everyone hung out listening to the radio on porches, drinking beer and smoking cigarettes. The men wore white t-shirts and bermuda shorts, the women pink halter tops and jogging pants. At night there were barbecues. People dropped in on each other.

Sometimes, if we could tear her away from the track, we'd take Mrs. E to a ball game, even if the Yankees were in town. Then we'd come home to a pot roast or ham cooked by J.D. in honor of Jane's return. We'd watch TV and drink cans of cheap beer and after a while friends of the family would come by to smoke joints and play old records. They'd tell stories about seeing Little Stevie Wonder and The Supremes at summer fairs, but also about strikes and the riots. Sometimes we'd dance, and Jane'd play guitar. Usually the night would end with Mrs. E sitting on my lap, trying to make out. Those days were the best.

Jane called her Ma, stretching the sound out to three syllables, if she was mad. Otherwise it was, "Norma, git yer hands outta my hair." Like that.

Jane's childhood was lousy. Her parents loved her and her father always had a job at the plant, but they were in debt all the time and were forced to move around a lot during lay-offs. She had an uncle who molested her from the time she was three till she was seven, when it was his turn to go to war. He was blown to bits. They mailed his teeth and dog tags home for burial.

It was a funny kind of neighborhood. Jane's cousins owned a grocery there, and it was always getting robbed. Even with the big Doberman. Even with the twelve gauge behind the counter. But you could walk down the street at night. Everyone knew everybody else. That didn't prevent the most incredible violence from breaking out all of a sudden. Most of it was domestic. You'd hear screams and breaking glass, maybe gunshots. Then the cops would show up. It was one of those places they like to come to cause they know they won't get killed. The drug gangs were gone. It was just poor people taking everything out on each other. A cop could make all his quotas without risking his ass.

Jane was the first person in her family to complete high school or go to college. They laughed at her when she moved to New York. That she didn't do much with her education made sense to them. And it didn't seem to bother her. It was a way to get out of that city, out of blue-collar hell. The biggest thing she took with her was a pathological fear of poverty. And I never met a person who could blow so much cash so fast. I would miss the annual trip to the industrial heartland.

JUST SAY NO
Carol Cavileer

My husband (who was six foot four, and mean) abused me and my children. I called the police, but they always told him to leave for a couple of days. He always came back promising to change.

We went to a Christian marriage counselor who told me to apologize to my husband every time my husband lost his temper. He said that I should love my husband more; and above all, should obey him.

But when my husband told me I had to become a Baptist, I refused. And when he humiliated me in public, I argued. And when he beat my son in the face with a rolled-up newspaper and told me that was discipline, I hit my husband with a frying pan.

When the Christian counseling failed to instill me with the proper attitude, my passive-aggressive, manic-depressive, pathological liar, post stress-disordered, schizoid personality type husband took me to see a psychiatrist.

I walked in, knees shaking, wondering what I would say, sat down. He wrote down information: name, age, occupation. Asked me how I'd pay. I told him Medicaid. He didn't like that, I could see. He didn't know that I knew he had lost his license once for Medicaid fraud: seeing patients for ten minutes, charging welfare for an hour.

He told me to count backwards quickly from one hundred subtracting seven every time. He said to name the last five presidents, he asked me if the government exists. He said that intellectually I was fine. He asked about my education. I said that I had dropped out at thirteen. He asked why, I said I didn't like school. That bothered him. He said we all can't do just what we like. I asked him if he liked what he was doing now, his job. He didn't want to answer, but I pressed and he admitted that no, he didn't like it, not a bit. I asked him what sense it made to spend so much time doing what you do not like. He said that sometimes people spend whole lifetimes doing what they do not like. I told him I went back and got my G.E.D. and a college degree. I said that I loved art, loved to create.

Told him about my writing: the book I wrote, the plays, short stories, poetry. Published? he asked. Yes. Making any money? Some, I said, not much. He said I needed help. He spoke of norms, spoke as if the word 'norm' were a holy word. Said I didn't fall within the norm. I said norms change, reminded him that what was accepted as the norm a hundred years ago is now rejected, and that today's norms will likewise be discarded in the future.

He said I was very clever. Intelligent, he said. But these words, his words, were just the melted butter in the pan he would later fry me in. He asked me about relationships. I said I had been victimized by the men I loved. Told him about the man who knocked out my front teeth while I was pregnant with his child. He said that it was my fault for being with a man like that. Words bit, I recoiled. He asked what my problem was; I started crying, said it was my husband. He abuses me, I said, I don't love him anymore. He shrugged and said some people stay married to people that they don't love all their lives... One of his norms, I thought.

I pictured my sculpture, the one that took me weeks to make... the sculpture of a woman, the one I was so proud of, the one my husband smashed against our bedroom wall until it was no more than a shapeless lump of clay.

Is this therapy? I asked, still crying. He said yes, and do you know your writing is no more than the toilet paper you wipe the crap of your life onto? He'd never read a single line I'd written! Flow of tears stopped dead, stomach turned to rock. Fuck you, I almost said. Is that what music is? I asked. Is that what paintings are?

Some, he said, then asked me to sign a paper giving him permission to medicate me, giving him the rights to my mind.

I just said no, walked out to the car, and told my husband I would be filing for divorce.

I NEVER MEANT TO
Sue A. Austin

You know, I never really wanted to have dinner with him
But as luck would have it, I went anyway
It was the last thing on my mind
Something I had no excitement to do
And as we talked, my thoughts freely circled the planet
Clearly, I didn't want to be here with this man.
In an endless effort to be kind,
I stopped my interplanetary travels to
Comment and add a supportive nod now and then
But quickly back into space I went
Seeking a retreat from my chattering comrade.
Droning on and on, did I know this or that
I cut short my mental trip
Making a rough landing, I was back to reality
You know, I never meant to have dinner
With this man that I married.

BILLY
David Jewell

The trailer park is killing me—like the machine at the bowling alley—the long arm that slides and knocks all the standing pins down and sets up different ones in their place... you know what I mean.

And Babe ain't lookin' too happy staring at the TV all day watching Oprah and Phil talk all their fucking nonsense... it gives her ideas... and when I get home she asks why I can't be one of those more sensitive men... and I tell her why don't she shut up and get a goddamn job.

She's starting to get fat from all those little cans of Schlitz malt liquor she keeps popping down. She says they're just little cans and there ain't much in them so she drinks three times as many.

I'm not getting paid enough at the filling station...that's easy to figure out. I get home and I'm greasy and Babe looks at me for about two seconds through the fuzz of her TV eyes like I'm just a channel she switched to and then switched away from... then her dog starts barking and I swear one of these days I'm gonna stuff it through the TV screen and throw the whole damn thing out the window.

Babe and me had some pretty good times a long time ago, but that was a long time ago and if things don't get better pretty soon I don't know... that's why I'm here... that's why I'm ready to rob this convenience store and get our butts to Mexico that should change a couple of things.... that should shake it up.

I reach in the glove compartment to get the gun, put it in my jacket pocket and walk into the 7-11. Nobody else is in here, nobody for miles around. I look at the guy behind the counter and nod. He says—Howdy Do—or some crap like that. He's an old guy. Looks like somebody's daddy. Got a wedding ring and a weird haircut, like his daughter gave it to him, trying to make him look stylish, even though it's way too late for him to worry about that shit.

I walk to the beer section and stare at all that beer. It's cold back there. I don't like it. The lights make me feel like I'm in an operating room and a picture flashes of the old man stretched out on a table while the doctors try to keep his heart going long enough to pull the bullet out that I'm going to put into him. Maybe more than one bullet.

My hand is in my jacket pocket, fooling around with the gun, switching the safety On & Off... On & Off. The handle feels good, rough, cool, covered with a bunch of little bumps to give me a better grip. I keep staring at all the beer. I want to shoot something. I want to shoot all those cans of Schlitz malt liquor... shoot that fucking bull between the eyes.

"Is there anything I can help you with back there?"

And I think, yeah, hand the money over peaceful so I don't have to blow your fucking brains out and mess up your goddamn haircut. But I just say, "No. Can't decide what kind of beer to buy is all."

"There's a special on Busch."

"Land of the Sky Blue Waters."

"No, that's Hamm's Draft. Busch. Now I don't know where it comes from. They don't show them beer ads on TV like they used to."

"Right..... jesus..."

How am I gonna pop this old geezer? How am I gonna pop this old pop? I wonder how much money he's got over there anyway. 7-11, what the hell is this place? This is hell in here. Hell... with the air-conditioner too high and the lights too bright. And I don't want a beer.... I do want something.... but I don't think they sell it in here. Damn.

"Pretty hot night for September, ain't it?"

"It's pretty hot outside..."

"What's that?"

"It's fucking freezing in here."

"Har har har... Wouldn't you know it!"

Fuck it. I can't shoot this guy. What'd he ever do to me? He ain't the one keeping me down. It's them rich bitches up in them hills powdering each other's asses all day is why I'm stuck in that fucking trailer watching Babe watching Phil and Geraldo... Shee-it.

I go to the counter and ask for Marlboro Reds in a box and put down three dollars.

"Decided against the beer, didya? O.K. Let's see...."

And then he starts fucking around with the register, like he just saw it for the first time, like it just materialized in front of his face.

"That ain't all I decided against."

"What's that?"

"Never mind...."

Then I walk out the door... listening to the door buzzer... feeling like it's inside my head... knowing I have to go home and tell Babe I don't have the money, while the dog barks its stupid head off.

PNB
(DEC. 31-1986, 2326HRS.)
W.H. Steigerwaldt

The investigator and I
are dispatched
to a local motel bar
full of New Years revelry
and a pulseless non-breather.

Upon our arrival we
find a large crowd
standing in a circle
speculating loudly
about a great,
fat, white male,
laying on the floor
amid them,
whose skin is already
chalky looking
with death.

Brian barks into his
portable "get an
ambulance here fast"
as I kneel next to the
man, probe for pulse,
look for breath.

My partner rips the
victim's vomit stained
shirt open and sez,
"Bill, I'll pump."

I nod and arc the man's
head back.
I'll do the breath.

Brian furiously begins
to press at the sternum,
counting his one-onethousand,
two-onethousand,
beginning the rhythm.

After the
five-onethousand
I try to seal the
man's lips with mine
and give a full
lung of breath.

As I do so I am
met with a great
font of Cheeto, beer,
and peppermint schnapps
flavored
vomit,
the man's last meal.

I spit out the hash
as Brian pumps again.
I begin to scoop
the mess out of the
mouth before me...
...try again at
the breath...
....a repeat of the same.
I am gagging,
spitting, eyes watering.

Brian begins the
rhythm again,
but our glances
tell us that it's useless...
he has aspirated...
packed full.

The ambulance crew
arrives after too
many minutes
of this.

They take over.

While I wash my
mouth out at
a drinking fountain,
I hear a drunken voice
slurring, "you fuckin' cops
killed him, you killed him,
you assholes don't know
what you're doin'."

Without responding
I turn to the stairwell,
follow the EMS crew
outside.

My suspicions have
been confirmed.
$7.35 an hour
just isn't enough.

Happy New Year.

THE FILCHED "FRONTIER"

"When you put the finishing stroke on that painting, I knew something was going to happen..." he said, and I imagined a spray-can weilding vandal protecting his homophobia.

O.K. so I did this homoerotic painting of Kirk and Spock. It's kinda what I do - paint erotica ... pornography to you in the burbs. And I grew up next door to book burners in Virginia, so I should have known ....

Invited to show my paintings at a university art gallery in Oregon, I shipped off everything I had. And then the call came - that one that makes your stomache leap out of your throat and run around the room going "Aye Aye Aye Aye Aye Aye." MY painting was GONE!

"I DON'T KNOW HOW TO TELL YOU THIS... BUT SOMEONE STOLE 'THE FINAL FRONTIER!' "

"OMIGODOHCHRIST OHSHIT YOUMUST BEJOKINGNOWAY OH SHIT OH SHIT!"

BRING ME THE HEAD of "STAR TREK BOY"

Despite incredible feelings of **HOSTILITY**, we went up for the opening.

Driving into town, everyone I looked at was suspect. "THAT COULD BE THE GUY WHO STOLE MY PAINTING! OR THOSE KIDS OVER THERE! — OR THAT GIRL!"

However, my aggression was quickly melted by the overwhelming sea of regrets and apologies at the opening. The entire town was disemboweling itself with embarrassment that THIS could have happened on their soil.

After having the same conversation over and over again...

"I'M SO SORRY ABOUT YOUR PAINTING!"

"YEAH, me too."

... we fled with some friendly locals to do a pub crawl and get loaded.

During these well lubricated discussions, everyone seemed to agree that the prime suspect was one "STAR TREK BOY," a strange lurking figure without a real name, who's only discerning feature was an obvious fixation with the T.V. show.

But no one had a CLUE where he lived or who he was ....

The next thing I knew, I was flying to Virginia. My grandmother had died in bed, listening to talk radio, with a bag of cookies.

DEATH of a Glamour Queen

Lilla was a wanna-be movie star gone haywire. Over the course of a lifetime of disappointment and unrealized dreams, she retreated into a dismal, lonely world of booze and anti-depressants. Budweiser and Xanax speedballs. And she would do anything in her power to pull you in there with her. An Icelandic beauty who never got her shot at Hollywood, it was dismally sad and fascinating to read her old school notebooks, where she practiced her English phrases "WOULD YOU LIKE SOME TEA?" "YES, I WOULD LIKE SOME TEA." and cram page after page with lists of movie star's names "Ida Lupino, Joan Crawford, Betty Davis..."

Lilla's nearest brush with fame was being one of the sea of people fleeing Egypt in "The Ten Commandments"... let my people go, and all that. I always look for her and NEVER find her. Then there was the tantalizing offer to be an "Errol Carol" girl. He scouted out good looking gals to parade around his Hollywood club, dressed in EXTRAVAGANT costumes ... very "Folies Bergères." But grandpa said "ME AND THE KID, OR HOLLYWOOD. NOT BOTH." And so, off to the burbs.

☆ Lilla ☆

The same woman who had given me her plastic "snake-skin" miniskirt to wear in high school could also be INCREDIBLY brittle and FRIGHTENING. Booze made holidays into dizzying scream-fests or soggy sentimental pits of melancholy. She was fickle, demanding, narcissistic, manipulative and wonderful. Once when she was strung out on her prescription drug of choice, she threw away all her address + phone books. Everyone was a "SON-OF-A-BITCH." Except for me and Marcos. And we were suddenly LIVING WITH HER. INVISIBLE. FOUR-YEARS OLD.

So she didn't need our number in California any-more...

Strange Tales of Fear and STUPIDITY

Meanwhile, up in Oregon, a BOIL had been festering in the fermented brain of a local woman. Posters that were put up to advertise the theft of the painting had resulted in it's MYSTERIOUS RETURN, wrapped in grocery bag paper. Perhaps "Star Trek Boy" had realized what my friend Dave had said: "A REAL TREK FAN WOULD NEVER STEAL." Or possibly my tear-jerking poster just made someone feel bad. Unfortunately, it also resulted in this woman going RABID, ripping down the posters and launching a one-woman campaign. She brought her complaint to the University faculty, who didn't give her SATISFACTION. She was BOOED out of a campus meeting, then went to the Dean. Nothing. By now no doubt foaming at the mouth, she called the local papers, all too eager to lend their pages to her cause, her Senators and Congressmen, and various organizations formed to outlaw homosexuality, seal mouths and eyes, and send us all into the Dark Ages. She even tried to get Paramount to sue me. CHARMING.

Oddly, nothing really happened. Paramount seems to have bigger fish to fry, and her attempts to have the gallery closed have, so far, been fruitless. Things are getting back to "normal."

CHINA WHITE
Bana Witt

I'd finally given-up on my battered 280Z, which had begun to look like crumpled aluminum foil, when the clutch went out. A heavy metal bass player I knew was selling his Ford V-8 pick-em-up truck and after I drove it around for a few days, I became delirious with power and bought it.

For some reason I'd driven this truck over from Oakland, where I was living, to the City and ended up in North Beach with my big woolly wild poet friend David.

There was this other older poet David knew who had just gotten back from the Golden Triangle, where he had written a hundred and one vignettes to the opium poppy. They weren't fast moving pieces, but he had been coming to the reading series at Bannam Alley to share them. Somehow even the poorest North Beach poets seem to be able to teleport themselves to exotic and distance places at will.

He'd brought back a bunch of really pure white heroin called China White and he and his wife had returned with big habits. Poets were nodding out all over town because this guy was so generous.

I never spent much time in North Beach, as I'm not very good at hanging-out and most of those people are world class. I can't stay up late and don't drink or put-out anymore, so really, what's the point?

Anyway David had heard that the old traveling poet had been giving serious amounts of this heroin to friends who didn't even have habits, and this skinny poet named Paul had been given more than he knew what to do with and was willing to share.

So we trudged up some impossibly steep hills and many concrete stairs and then more vertical wooden stairs and ended up at a monastic flat of ancient Beat origins. The place was clean and sparse even though he'd lived there for years.

Paul offered us both tiny white lines of powder. I hadn't even tried any of the stuff in ten or twelve years and that had been Mexican and had made me very sick. But this, this China White, was the stuff of Junkie legend, and I'd never tried it, so I snorted some. David did a second line a few minutes later, but I didn't.

Right as we had really started coming on and I was beginning to loose my balance, our host said, "You know, you guys have to split because my old lady's coming home and she doesn't know I have this stuff and I really don't want her to find out."

I looked at David in half-lidded shock. Getting horizontal was the only movement I was ready for. All stationary lines had become unstable. As I peered down the abyss that was the stairwell, I breathed deeply, moved slowly and slid my sweaty hand down the worn bannister; trying hard to concentrate; trying hard to ignore the fact that the warm Jello in my knees had begun to liquefy.

David was doing quite well, he wanted to go to City Lights bookstore. I tried to be tough but asked to hold onto him. I gripped his arm like a last brief connection to the tangible world.

We had two more treacherous blocks to descend, waves of nausea began to ripple through my body, the cool night air tried to soothe me, but I was having none of it.

When we got to City Lights I sat down on the curb, telling David to go on in. I'd wait there. He went inside and my stomach heaved. I began to projectile vomit into the street. A deep, loud and profound retching that sounded like my body trying to forcibly evict my soul. People gave wide berth to my crumpled form. I felt fine. I didn't mind.

David emerged with a book in hand. He told me I looked terrible and asked me if I was all right. I said no, but somehow I didn't care. And he said, "Let's go to Caffe Trieste," and I walked fragilely along, hoping vaguely for even pavement.

We oozed into the cafe and my face began pouring sweat. I sat down and made a feeble attempt to look coherent. I had several dramatic bouts of fervent prayer before the porcelain shrine in the bathroom and told David I had to lie down, soon. My body was getting angrier and angrier at me for this latest betrayal.

I asked David if he'd drive me home to Oakland, as he seemed able to maintain, having a long opiated background and a very big tolerance because of his size.

Slowly, he led me to my truck as I puked my way through North Beach. Once we got on the Embarcadero Freeway I rolled down the window, hanging my head out in the wind like a dog. After we got onto 580 I began to barf again. It streaked the side of the truck and caused alert motorists to change lanes.

David said he'd never seen anyone get quite this sick and that maybe I had an allergy to opiates.

"Maybe," I replied, as I disgorged more digestive juices toward a passing stationwagon.

We made it to my house and David slept on the floor in the living room in case I died or something.

Whenever someone asks me if I want to do some heroin and I tell them that it makes me throw up and they say, "It does that to everyone," and I say, "Yeah, sure, catch me next time," and go home to my dog.

THE SHOW GOES ON
David West

After making movies, singing, acting, and doing countless drag
extravaganzas from Australia to San Francisco, Doris Fish died of AIDS
on June 22, 1991. A benefit held before her death was called, *Who Does
That Bitch Think She Is?*

I've known men so terrified
of who they grew up to be
their bodies are worse than prisons
& I've seen my share of elegant victories
over the male bastille
all it takes is style & the courage to insist
Doris even made it look graceful
when her hair fell out she had wigs for days
love has never needed a license to exist
the show goes on. the tide will change
but it keeps taking the best we have with it
old men with your stone tablets
let the pecking order beware
Doris Fish is dead but her drag's still here

once upon a time, in California friends
when I was hired as the token queer
at a politically correct hippyshit grocery store
I found myself necking in the dairy cooler
with a girl, thinking: what will I say
if someone sees us? I didn't seem to fit in anywhere
and I wasn't sure I should
I couldn't swing that .45 caliber conception
of men who are sexy depending on how many holes
they can blow in their victims
Doris's sluts-a-go-go were more fun

than Sylvester Stallone & I think a laugh
is more persuasive than a gun
Doris is dead but the show goes on

there's a difference
between the direction of the wind and a trend
between accidents and tragedies, attitudes and men
between going down on someone and coming back up again
it takes all kinds of grace to sustain us
Doris fell off a balcony in a show one time
and kept singing while she hung to the rail
I see her face on the moon and get mad again
she'll never even be on a postage stamp—hell,
 the first man the U.S. put in orbit also launched
a political career that ended in a banking scam
he got a postage stamp—I'll vote for Doris she was my kind of man
she had demands but they were very modest

go down Moses, leave the commandments alone
the promised land is a safe place to sleep
it's the freedom to make your way home, unmolested
loaded, in heels and gold lamé, at 3 a.m.
lord have mercy on the extravagant of spirit
when boys drive by in muscle cars, not applauding
you haven't lived till you've seen
her housefrau in curlers, her dumb blonde
but I'm smarter than you routine
Doris made me happy her wit was so crisp
doing sexual jujitsu on those old hollywood roles

I like to imagine Doris walking down main street
in small town USA at high noon, disturbing
what passes for the peace these days
and I think it's even harder to change people

than the law: I want Doris on prime time TV
I've met children 10 years old
who already learned how to whisper faggot
I've been so sick of it I saw myself
sprawled on the sidewalk with a cup and a sign
that says another sensitive soul who couldn't hack it
can you spare a quarter? I need a new dress

Doris is dead & I'm not depressed, I've had it
this is insane. she's on the front page
in all her former health & glory
right next to a budget cutback story
they keep the army in the closet
they keep playing with their guns, fighting the most
ridiculous wars you ever heard of and Doris is dead
couldn't a few missile silos disappear in her honor?
couldn't the president just admit on the news tonight
he doesn't know what he's doing and if we knew
what he was doing, we'd shoot him? Doris died
we have a plague on our hands
goddamn it we have a problem

Doris you can't leave we need you now
Schwarzenegger has his eye on the senate
Bush spent more money on one gulf war
than was spent on all medical research
in the world combined since the century began
 I get up and go to work in the morning
& even the Marlboro man looks sad
how many must follow her? how long will it take?
she was the queen of Vegas in outerspace
a pro, one of the best in the biz
Doris died how dare she we needed her bad
who does that bitch think she is?

DON'S KIDS
Violet

When I was sixteen my friend Leif and I were almost brothers, except for the fact that we didn't have the same parents, but none of our friends knew. It was the summer and we mostly hung around older kids in the small punk scene that Hawaii had. They drove cars while we rode our skateboards to get where we needed to go.

We met someone special on one of our attempts to buy some acid from the local neighborhood dealer kids, the Corso brothers: Frank, John, and Chris. Frank was an alcoholic that drove his moped into a wall at eighty miles an hour one night and had a hard time talking, and if you called him Francis you'd be dead within the week. John was around eighteen and could skate like a pro and had just about every thirteen-year-old punk girl sucking his dick. Chris was our age and was really fucking hot, he looked like a dark-haired Macauley Culkin, his eyes were always almost closed from all the pot he smoked. So Leif and I get to the Corso's place with Chris.

When we walk in the front door his mom is sitting on the couch smoking a cigarette and watching soap operas while all their canaries are out of their cages, flying all over the house, shitting on stuff. The carpet is layered with yellowed newspapers, covered in canary shit which we have to walk on to get to Chris's room. He takes out a half a sheet of blotter acid from this battered *Dukes of Hazzard* lunchbox. Leif and I get six hits between the two of us and then go back out front to skate on this ramp we built a few days before.

We're in the middle of the street when we see this beige American car pull up next to us. This man sticks his head out the window. "Hi, boys. It sure is hot today. Feel free to come on over to my place for a refreshment." He honks his horn twice and pulls into the driveway of this brown paneled townhouse.

"Hey, Chris, who is that guy?"

"Yeah, Chris, he looks like Mr. McFeely, the mailman from *Mr. Roger's Neighborhood*."

"That's Don. He likes young boys. He's a little weird but he's cool. He gives you drinks if you hang out with him."

"Let's go."

So the three of us go up to his house and ring his doorbell. He comes to the door wearing a button-up shirt with sweat splotches under the arms. "I'm glad you boys decided to come over. Come on in."

We follow him into his living room and sit side by side on his couch. The thing's made out of a horrible color of that stuff that cheap stuffed animals are wrapped in. "Hey, boys, I'm going to go whip up some refreshments, so you can watch this video while I'm in the kitchen."

He has one of those old, wood-paneled VHS machines that you load on the top. He pulls a video out of his bookshelf and stuffs it in. He does all this while talking in his kind of timid voice. "So, Chris, who are your two friends?"

Chris introduces Leif and me, and Don responds with an enthusiastic "Nice to meet you." The video is a porno film with this girl standing naked on a glass table and taking a shit on it while she fucks herself with this big pink dildo. Under the table is a fat shaved man jerking off to the image of shit falling in front of his protected face.

Don comes back out into the living room with a tray holding four glasses and a blender filled to the top. "You boys like strawberry daiquiris? This will cool us off." He pours us our cups and sits back in his chair. "It sure is hot today, don't you think?"

We all look at each other and Chris agrees. Don starts to undo the top buttons of his shirt and scratches his furry chest. "How do you boys like the movie?"

"It's weird. Who the fuck would want to get shit on?"

"Some people are into strange things, Leif."

We finish up our cups when Don says that he'll go make more if we take our shirts off. We do and he stares for a few seconds before going back into the kitchen. "Chris, what's up with that guy?"

"He likes to have young boys get naked while he keeps giving them strawberry daiquiris. You can do more if you want. I let him take pictures of me in exchange for money or stuff. Last week he bought me a new skateboard."

"I thought you made money from selling acid."

"No, my brother keeps all the money, I just get acid for free." Don comes back with another pitcher full, pours us all another round and takes his shirt off. I don't know what I'm doing here but I'm really drunk. When the video ends, he gets up and tells us he's got some phone calls to make but wants to know if we want to come back tomorrow around the same time. While we put our t-shirts back on, he offers us these porn magazines he supposedly gets free because of his job. After we're let out we skate down the street as Chris mumbles something about how Don is the manager of a bookstore downtown.

The next day goes the same way. We show up as he throws on a video and brings us strawberry daiquiris. By the time he has us down to our underwear I can see his hard-on through his pants. I start to get hard because I've never seen so much of Chris's skin before. I notice Chris is hard too. Leif is just kind of watching the TV with a drunken stare. Don asks us how much money we would want if we let him take pictures of us while we had sex with each other. I look at Chris who says a hundred each. Leif and I agree as we get out of our underwear. Don says okay. The three of us look surprised as we all get on the carpet and start to touch each other's chests. Chris twists his face at mine and we start kissing. It's like kissing a girl since he hasn't started to shave yet. We slosh our tongues around together and grab each other's cocks and start jerking them off. In the corner of my eye Leif is watching us and jerking off as well. It was obvious that Chris and I were going to be the main subject. Our kiss broke and we spun around putting our dicks in each other's face. I was on top and all I saw was Chris's cock. It was thin, like a pencil with one blue vein running up the side. The head was pink and turned-up just like his nose. I held his balls in one hand and sucked on his dick. I guess it was easy to deep throat since it was so tiny. I could smell the sweat between his legs and feel his pubic hair when my lips got to the base. With my other hand I rubbed the saliva that trickled down to his asshole in circles and slid in my index finger and started fucking it. We came at the same time. I felt his come hit the back of my throat and pulled his dick out of my mouth so I could see it. Come spilled down my fingers as I milked it for all I could get then licked it off my fingers.

We got up on our knees and kissed. Leif had come on the carpet and Don had his cock in one hand and seemed to have videotaped the whole thing. After we all got dressed, he explained that he wasn't going to show the video to anybody, he just wanted it for himself. We collected our money and continued to go back to Don's house on a weekly basis. It felt real hot to lose my virginity to Chris. Leif didn't go back again, only Chris and I would. We didn't have to touch Don and besides it was cool to get a hundred dollars for letting some guy just watch.

One day while Don was in the kitchen fixing us sandwiches we took the video of us and stashed it in Chris's backpack. We had a good time that day. Chris fucked me in the ass with his hard little dick and came all over my back. Don told us, "Since the both of you are like sons to me..." He had a big surprise for us out in the garage. When we got there we saw two brand new Beach Cruiser bicycles. One black, one red. "No way! Are these for us?"

"Yeah, boys, I thought you might be tired of riding around on those skateboards." We gave him a hug and thanked him on our way out then rode our new bikes all the way back to my house, doing wheelies and screaming "FUCK" at every car we passed. We watched the video of ourselves and got so turned on that we ended up fucking again.

We spent the next four days at my house watching videos, getting stoned and fucking. The both of us were paranoid that other people in our scene would freak out if they knew that Chris and I were boyfriends. Chris didn't want his brothers to find out because they would kick his ass. I wasn't too concerned though, because most everyone thought I was kind of queenie for wearing eyeliner and occasional lipstick. So after about a quarter ounce of pot and a hundred orgasms we agreed on going back to his house to get some drugs to sell at this party going on that same night.

When we turned the corner of Chris's street there were at least a dozen police cars parked. At first we thought that his brother's drug ring got busted but it turned out that all the police were going in and out of Don's house. A bunch of people were all standing around talking to each other under their breaths. I asked this woman what was going on. She said that some kid had complained to his parents about Don. The kid said Don had taken pictures of him naked and got him drunk on strawberry daiquiris that he thought were just smoothies or something, that he wasn't the only one, Don had lots of kids come over.

A cop came up to us and asked if we knew anything about Don, if we were ever over to his house for drinks, and had he ever touched us. Of course, we said no when the cops turned around to see Don escorted out the front door of his house. Neighbors were yelling out insults and a few eggs were thrown. Why would we ever want to help our friend get busted, even if he was getting busted anyway? Don looked at us as he was getting into the back of a police car with a bit of apology and self-pity wrapped up into a blink of an eye.

Later that night, after everything was calm, we went across the street and broke into Don's house. When we got inside it was obvious that they tore the place up. All his videos were gone. We went down the hall, into the part of the house we hadn't been to. There were Keane prints framed and hanging on the walls. In the study a Norman Rockwell painting of young boys hung crooked over his desk. All his things had been messed with. We dug through the drawers ourselves and found notebooks, calculators, pocketbooks, all kinds of miscellaneous stuff with neon orange stickers labeling them. The stickers were circles with the letter D on each one. There was a roll of them in the top drawer. I guess he put them on his stuff, so people would know it was his. So we took it and left.

Later that week everyone was talking about it. All the kids called the house "Don's Porno Palace" and referred to him as "Strawberry Daiquiri Man." Chris and I told all the kids about the stickers and gave them out to anyone who said they knew Don. We put them on our skateboards, bikes, even over the circles that were on our Converse shoes. When people asked us what it meant we simply told them, "We're Don's kids."

FRATHOUSE BLUES
Trebor Healey

They told me it was about brotherhood
but mostly it was a dubious dabbling in drunk-drivin deliriums
doped up and holed up behind a great cement dam
entombed in the nursery of the straight white male hydroelectric
powerplant
Daddy turned all the levers
these were the princes of the powerbrokers
drunk, dumb and dosed
in the dungeons of consciousness

And I was running from queer demons
hidin behind walls as thick as these
—they had to be safe
hid among the big whining dynamos of electrical boysex
generatin the glowing germs of desire
like fireflies I couldn't *not see*
I ran in place for four years
impressed by turbines and flumes
Drunken I debated delicious dick dichotomy
convinced myself it was envy for their sex not greed for it
lost every case
and was sentenced by my penis to hard labor
in a fraternity
I was in a prison made of my own passion
the bars ah my cell
were big hard blue-veined cocks
I shook em and I wailed
for release

My dreams were kinder to me though
flowering like the blossoms of hard dicks
floatin like lotus flowers on a warm white sea of fresh boy cum
flowin from the frightened eyes of these sexy scared boys even
who cried subconsciously for me
—I know they did
they cried for me and they cried for themselves
we cried in brotherhood without ever lettin on
for the boy in us all
that was killed when the bell of initiation into this frat manhood
thing rang
That was the only brotherhood we really ever had
a brotherhood of loss
like our dicks setting down like the sun
when they coulda drove deep and found a place to swim upstream
upstream where the river still ran wild
and none of em ever knew
that I sauntered in a solitary
subversion of semen somnambulance
cuz I was a fag

I'd say it was a heaven
but delicious dick dichotomy determined
it was purgatory
They had these things called brotherhoods
in which they dominated the new pledges
the older boys made us strip and do calisthenics
we were so close
to just letting it go
the room was full of sweat and groaning
so close to realizing my fantasies
and maybe a few others'
We woulda done anything the older boys said
to achieve brotherhood

We woulda paired up and fucked each other all night
for brotherhood
We woulda got on our knees for the older guys we so wanted
approval from
for brotherhood
We woulda let em fuck us and welcome us home
We woulda sucked each other's 18-year-old stems
for brotherhood
For Brotherhood
we woulda cummed for distance
instead of vomiting for distance
Ain't it the same thing sublimated?
I mean four years of watching these guys guzzle beer
it always seemed like they were trying to prove to one another
what great cocksuckers
they coulda been
how much they could take
Like randy Marlon Brandos on the waterfront:
"I coulda been a cocksucker
You shoulda watched out for me Charlie
—you was my brother."
        Brotherhood

And I felt sorry for em
trapped behind that Hoover Dam
that made em strive for fifty-two years
their Daddy's age, stamped on the fuselage of a B-52 bomber
the age of power and privilege
not a place for boys or cocksuckers

They told me the frat would make me a man
And I thought Good!
cuz I'm slippin into womanhood real fast
        Oh, when does a boy become a man?
When he signs a contract of brotherhood he plans to break?
When he stops caring about words having meaning?

When he accepts 'I'm a Zete' as a tag of brotherhood
simply because it has status and the love be damned
When he decides once and for all to bow down to Daddy
and suck the dick of his dogma instead of the dick of his friend?
—It was happening before my eyes too soon
They were teensomething, twentysomething young guys
When does a boy become a man?
As soon as his cock drops I'd say
droppin into manhood
every one of em
like virile bombs outta the lumbering B-52s that were their fathers
cuz they couldn't find brotherhood
no one had shown them a way
And I coulda but was afraid

And crossing the river Styx was the first trial most woulda turned
from
Our sticks straining together forcing the pussywillow off the bough
and into a fabulous fellatiated flower full ah pollen
For brotherhood I longed
even lied   with them
For Brotherhood
Oh so close
to lie with them is only a conjugation away
like the rules of language
the rules of the fathers kept our dicks apart
But still for brotherhood I longed
It's what they promised me you know
I who would never fit in
I knew how to be a brother to them
I was the only one who knew

I was silent
and they told me over and over again
because I was a lie of what they were
and that made them trust me

They kept telling me how well I fit in
Their steelvault hearts I see even today on the streets of this city
10 years later
they coulda broken like eggs full ah semen
they coulda been take-off-that-tie sloppy and sticky
in boy-rompin randiness
They didn't have to be fags forever
for brotherhood

Youth wasn't worth shit
to these beautiful Adonises
women didn't want it
and their fathers laughed at it
considered it a liability
like a flower was somehow a necessary evil preceding a fruit
They couldn't bear their mother's love
how she thought they were cute
It compromised them into powerless obscurity
So they pretended to prefer the patriarchy's practicality about
produce
think that fags and mothers are the only ones who love them for
what they are
Beautified little boys unbeknownst
bearin their beautiful boners
like bamboo and bougainvillea

Power was all they were provided as a goal
So pansies and petunias be damned
They played their volleyball games
they got their grades and connections for grad school
they harvested their friendships and their fathers
they got their muscles all hard and tight
sleek as machinery
not for the girls
but for the other boys
for power over other boys

for intimidation
for a kind of hierarchy
My dick is bigger than yours kinda thing
got more horses ah power under my hood
A kinda brotherhood
and that's all a big dick was
a pecking order
For brotherhood
as in older brother and younger brother

Was it a fascination with something that they couldn't have?
The whole man-frat thing sure was for me
It was the central theme of my queer childhood
Before I knew what these feelings were
there were feelings of longing to be another little boy
I wanted to be the beautiful blond baseball battin boy
til my hairless little cock
stood straight up and pointed at him
"That one there; that's who you want to be"
I remember crying very long in my bed one night
when I was only 7
when I accepted that I would give up my family,
my room, all my toys and all my friends
—and Jesus too
to be that boy
I had three brothers who hated my guts
they would've loved that little blond boy
I couldn't be

No wonder it was sadness I saw
when I first looked upon my male seed in my hand
I'd missed my mark
Oh, if my penis had been a boy-seeking missile
or a bird of prey boy-bound

So the frat was a twisted sort of blessing

like a nest I'd stumbled into
and all that longing came back
a dormant seed watered by alcohol in drunken reverie
A nest of beautiful bacchanalian boyness
A cock nest
they were working like bees
honeycombin the college
with hexagonal cum compartments as they masturbated
in bathroom stalls and the private cubicles of the library
I wished then my asshole was six-sided
Oh, Cinderella lonely queer I'd long
if the cock fits, wear it
I dreamed one might be my prince
but I knew   I knew
we all were princes and we all fit each other perfectly
For brotherhood I longed
The brotherhood they'd each accepted initiation into
And I couldn't just offer up my toys and Jesus and family anymore
my hairless little dick
was a loaded .357 magnum now
and my desires felt dangerous

For true brotherhood
the things I coulda shown em
the fields of wildflowers non-fruit-bearing I coulda led em through
we were all the same age
generally the same size and strength
A big dick and a smaller one are not that different
in the grand scheme of things now are they?
Not among brothers
in the grand scheme ah things
like stars and liberty
equality and fraternity
For brotherhood carries no judgment
Brotherhood does mean love you know
a kind they were afraid of

And yet it was what this living arrangement was supposed to be
about
Was it a fascination then with something that they couldn't have
that made them talk about it and claim they had it
like how the African American girls straightened their hair
the sissies lifted weights to look like football stars
And me
I joined a fraternity to be a straight boy
and convince myself everything would be OK
and I will find protection
from losing the love of my family and friends
and all strangers
which I know I must die if I lose

Were they trying to prove that they could actually be a team?
like all the rulers had told them to be but failed
for competition was the priority always
and if the team didn't serve that
well no one gets rich at a co-op
Their teams are more like alliances I guess
NATO and all that, a common enemy
But real brotherhood—it bankrupted enmity
so brotherhood was relegated to language alone
They were trained to fight, fight, fight
even for brotherhood they were told
Alone, afraid, loading rifles of manproof
Oh, I would say again we had a brotherhood in this way
I was there too protectin my fragile manhood slippin away
they never knew
my sexual subversions
they too walked in a solitary semen somnambulance
their life asleep in their testicles

And all I could imagine
as I watched their lips pronounce it:
"fit"

How would I fit in each of them
in their assholes, in their mouths
How well all of them could fit and fill me
fit and fill each other
Oh brothers
I dreamed of wild fucking orgies
And I no longer believe they were an impossibility
We all wanted brotherhood
For brotherhood
think we all could've given ourselves to one epiphany

But my dreams went limp and I left
    left with no memory of union
only an infinite repertoire of masturbation material
the steamy showers
and their half-hard boycocks risen from sleep
the tender lines of hair that vertically descended
between their bellies and their belts like Chinese writing
I was cheated of the same thing they were
so I'm not bitter
we wanted brotherhood
and none of us got it
and I see it in their eyes today
receded far inward beyond their gray suits
that have formlessly canceled their male beauty
behind a wall of shapeless fabric
that only speaks for the power of the man
not the boy-joy springloaded flowery semen stem
which I hope   *I do hope*
their wives can retrieve something of
as they race into middle age after the spoils
the kingmakers promised

I hug them now when I see them on the businessman's boydead
streets
It's a sort of brotherhood I think

that they can still let themselves touch
I hated them for years for refusing to touch me
until I thought of brotherhood and what it could be
And maybe I am the only one of us who knows
        I better get to work teachin

So now I feel a sad lost love for these boys
for what we intended together
even if we failed
we were all scared, brainwashed and runnin
lost in the deafenin deluge
of the whining dynamos of electrical boysex
generatin the glowing germs of desire
that made us blind and vulnerable to the dogma of B–52s
And how much like 52 they are today
but I know what hangs between their legs is always young
A penis is forever a boy
And when it rises like the sun
it gives the boy in the man away

So these so-called men
are always boys to me
hug them close
lean forward into their arms
and wish them well
give them my gift of brotherhood longed for
—Otherwise I'll long forever
and besides I know it's what they want
For brotherhood is how we met
and what we dreamed upon together
10 long years ago
For Brotherhood
I woulda mounted em and left them my seed
the gift of spring
like a lucky bag ah Indian corn
they could carry through the valley of death

of being a straight white male businessman
And I coulda used their lucky bag in those hard years too
Oh, and even if it's only the scrap metal
of a plane that crashed in a field of wildflowers
there is a kind of brotherhood still salvageable in their eyes
I lean forward and hold them
I wish them well as brothers

And at night in my dreams I fall backward into their arms
into the arms of 40 naked athletic boys alive
and scented with sweat
sittin on the young fine fence of 20 years give or take
I'll give
And bless the boyhood that still breathes in em

FOURTH OF JULY
Albert Huffstickler

Uncle Ed's nerves were shot.
He'd been through both world wars.
He lived behind us in a little cottage,
surviving on his pension check,
and on the Fourth of July he never came out.
Once I went to ask him something
and found him crouched in the corner,
eyes wide and vacant, his mouth drooling spit.
After that, I always went far down the street
to shoot off my fireworks.
Well, one notable Fourth, Uncle Ed came out.
I guess a man can take just so much,
Dressed in his World War II uniform,
he marched down the street to the fireworks stand,
bought a dozen cannon crackers, marched back,
lined them up in the driveway
and lit them one by one,
mouth set, never flinching at the roar;
then, with a nod to all and sundry, he turned,
marched back inside his house
and closed the door.

CHEMICAL MAN
Marc Olmsted

The moon behind the wire?

Do you believe everything moves 360°?

Billy stood in the white sheet of the mental ward talking to the black man who thought himself Satan. Billy thought himself Buddha.

He had walked into the L.A. police station having taken mushrooms, but this only feeding the PCP messiah breakdown, the full moon directly above with two rainbow rings of condensing mist. He was wearing a Bogart felt hat, one tennis shoe and one rubber thong, a towel as a sort of Hindu skirt, an Indian pajama shirt and lovebeads, pre-punk shades, a mop in his hand as a yippie staff, and a plastic flight bag full of books and trinkets he intended to show Chief Davis and the inevitable media god. First step in changing the world: enlighten the cops.

He sat down in the police station followed by three friends who had driven him there. They thought it was a prank. Zed thought Billy might even be enlightened. The cops gave him half an hour to leave. A black man asked for change and Billy handed him a twenty dollar bill. He chanted a Hare Krishna book in the cold white of the station, finally taken away in cuffs.

"You fools, you're playing right into my hands," he said.

A week earlier, fifth time of the drug. Lying on his bed, PCP dentist chair. The room hummed super-eight, the movie of his past unfolding from his brain. His long brown hair hung limp, delicate pale face beaded with chemical sweat. Divorced parents, Roman Catholic twisted smile, now in San Francisco film school to be Wells, Goddard, whoever.

Did he sleep that night, eyes hardly blinking in the room washed with passing headlamp glare?

Ancient past: chalice and Eucharist, sainthood abandoned. Even the Hindu period, a joke. Guilty mandala, in the center, a snap. He went to the airport, mysteriously uplifted, home for Xmas, saying goodbye to his girlfriend on the phone.

"You sound great," she said.

"I am."

The cops drove him to the Neuropsychiatric Ward over luminous L.A. freeways.

"Write a poem about us," they laughed.

He told the examining physician, "You're gay, I know. It's okay." The doctor seemed to blanch in the fluorescent night, trick or treat.

Thrown into the craziest ward with Black Satan, the burned-face hippie, the eight-months-pregnant young woman shouting at his Christ face, "I wanna get fucked!" The old man blubbering lips as he beat his chest mea culpa.

A young bad acid trip yelled it was the end of civilization, locked away in her dim ward. "The end, the end!"

"Only metaphysically," he said, whatever that meant.

Next day he knew Mother and Father would be there minutes before he saw them. Leaving the Rec Room of maniacs he predicted his parents through a small glass square in the metal door, a sort of vault or submarine effect - their faces of decompression. They entered.

He spoke soothingly to Mother, tying a piece of thread around her wrist to protect her from the CIA and demons. She wept. To Billy, they were tears of gratitude.

The ward. He awoke to find himself sane on the third day, the opposite of Christ. No ascension, back in mortal clay, soon led off by Dad and unable to resist telling the young psychiatrist, "Maybe you'll hear of me."

Sullen, horribly irritable in the car. Eager to return to his apartment in S.F., Dad wanting to know what happened.

"I guess you could call it a noble experiment gone wrong."

Dad was not pleased. The mocking shrine of L.A. autos. Billy went straight for the wine when Dad got him home.

"Maybe that's the problem," said Dad.

"O-hh-hh, Dad." Wouldn't you need a drink after falling from grace?

Smoked some more of the PCP as soon as he got back to S.F., the sweet menthol cool medicinal dentist taste of the drug spreading over him.

I salute the sun with one eye, o cyclopean pin head, o miracle of Satan and Jezuz, I march into the world with all the answers, I announce New Time, I correct the wicked.

Dish yer fault through the black plague, I've never had it! The blast church cunt rap zuch yer mithering sin.

He began the acid. It was school holiday for a month. Plenty of time to experiment. Nobly. Every day a sliver of the drug, not enough to make the mind forget its own skull, just enough for the blistering eye in the too-bright chemical joy, whew! Now wasn't *that* something whether dog on the street or skull in the head, but still knowing where the dog began and the skull ended. For a while.

Blag+Stooge! skullheap, fists of blood, murdering hoards of insect I was yer mother.

Ah and yes and o so very so he was back in the grip of the Almighty. And which Almighty? Whichever one you please and did it matter said the Nazi crossing himself in the ruined char.

As a teenager, he'd been initiated into the secrets of American Hindu, Hindoo madness, he joined the Mantra Club and after several years of devout mantra chanting flew to his guru and learned to teach it, finally giving up after a year when he felt as dumb as those who paid $35 a mantra (of which Billy got $17.50). But now, in the days of acid, he found himself suddenly as great as his guru, greater! Now the guru would clap his hands, so proud (for he undoubtedly knew all along, being a clever guru, that Billy was the Buddha to come, Maitreya), and the manic surge filled him like a slow motion atom cloud spreading over the Mojave in an orange flash, v-rooooooomm the dust spreads out and Billy didn't have to worry anymore. Billy was God and Krishna and Buddha back on Earth to help with the Marvel Comic war of Good vs. Evil Bhagavad Gita slugout where angels and demons, Olympian, Set and mighty Isis, the whole Justice League of America, Super-Jagger, Jaws, every last archetype returned to XX Century to pummel each other into shadow or light, the bone of the dice with the black hole cavities of luck, Shiva would win because all was Shiva, all a dream even if the planet went up in neutron dust, Shiva lit his joint in the void and took a galaxy.

He smiled in the dusk of his apartment. So good to know exactly what to do every moment down to the last toothbrush.

But must be careful, the CIA lurked everywhere. He dodged them on buses, he felt their shifty auras behind him, he challenged strangers with knowing looks, he abandoned his thoughts so as not to be traced, not even a fingernail could be left behind at the movies, elementals would get it and take it to the black magick CIA who already bombarded him with sinister dusts.

He decided to go to Santa Cruz and initiate old friends. He hitched down profound, a carpenter of future New Testament; here's the holy bum, gaining acid revelations seeing through time, ghosts of auto moved from parking lots as if future and present overlapped, scream frozen halfway into grin.

To arrive and find himself strangely down, ah the pain of the Son of Man, he had to sit in a field and chant his mantra to feel better, lonely. He returned to a party that afternoon where they gave him more acid in the dorms, beer, valium, coke, they gave him a rubber mask head to wear, o his antics, what they must've thought, encouraging him to greater hilarity, until finally Billy got the message and walked out zombie down to the dining hall and onto the auditorium stage to see the faces of everyone Olympian turning and leaving trails of their own superimposed auras, gods, devils, goddesses, hag demons, all chatting about the end of the world, and he, Maitreya, the Great Apologist for humankind, Jester rather than Saint on the Cross, times had changed but one still martyred to the cause, took off his clothes walking out across the tables. Go to applause.

Someone rushed out, some adult – some leader of the cafeteria – some cafeteria manager rushed up and yanked him from the dining table and he slumped in their arms as they dragged him into the playroom of pool tables and ping pong, and some hippie doctor said, "Relax, your body can't take it," so relax he did, closing his eyes, staring at the red pattern of the inner lids, then opening them slowly to "Easy, easy, easy." Suddenly a babe reborn into the maternity room, doctor staring down with gauze mask, "Easy, easy," and he fell through the blood-red of his own lids into the new body of himself in the playroom. The hippie doctor led him off to his near-campus pad but was a bit nasty once they were there, obviously bored with the behavior of young acid, and Billy excused himself in a seemingly saner condition. "Can I go now?"

The hippie doctor shrugged. Billy left.

But the campus police were alerted. Billy continued his madness, singing mantras in showers, accosting people with sexual overtones, then the campus police appeared to him like Atlantis storm troopers and he knelt before them. They took him away in the whirling red light machine, leaving him in the town.

Here it becomes difficult, how much more acid did he take, what made him start to wander the streets seeing a demon or a ghost or a god everywhere?

He cut his finger on his own razor, saying to the hippie he thought was Shiva, "You did that." The hippie said yeah.

He walked to a strange door and knocked on it. An old man answered.

"Do you know me?" asked Billy.

"No." The old man thinking on Manson and knives. Santa Cruz had more than its share of madness, Satanism, ritual murders.

"I thought you did," said Billy, spinning around and walking down the steps as the door slammed behind him.

I walk the work like Kung Fu I have lost my magick we're all reborn Atlantean magick kids and now it's time for me to lead.

Humble origins. I am the son of a character actor. Raised in L.A. I walk the plank of intuition. I scared everyone like Black Cloud Mulligan.

He walked across the mud of the little river and sank one foot into it, ah all so Cain-like as the dusk approached, and finally as he crossed it he saw in his fatigue some HELP CENTER or HOSPITAL it glowed its sign in the night like Shiva or Brahman or somebody big, outstandingly kind, we do understand...

To Billy it was heaven, he came to the glass doors and pressed the buzzer, nurses in the golden light inside came to the glass slowly, '40s heaven movie. They were very kind and he spoke to them as if they were angels and they brought him in, the nurses slowly realizing he was absolutely gone though he thought they understood. He talked to the old folks in their wheelchairs in the lobby, one was Madam Blavatsky, another Walt Whitman, or even Maharishi, maybe both at the same time, the archetypes blending and meshing, becoming one flesh.

One nurse called her boyfriend to bring a taxi for Billy and take him to the mental ward to save the ambulance expense. She asked, "What are you afraid of?"

Billy said, "Needles."

"Now you have to go away for a while," and he felt like Christ going into Hell to investigate after death freeing original sinners or some such Catechismal abysmal.

He entered the ward and they wondered if he were truly fucked up enough to lock away. This strange night crew of hippie doctors and nurses, young collegiate night shift, asked if he had anyone to call, but he was not quite able to remember phone numbers, so nobody to take him away, what were they going to do? He had an odd memory of the bearded doctor (was it in fact the same hippie doctor of Santa Cruz campus?) advancing towards him with a needle as if testing him, trying to freak him out, using the confession of his fear to the nurse? And Billy shrugged with his eyes if you want to crucify me go ahead to hell and they locked him in the outer lobby to discuss amongst themselves whether to put away Mr. William Moon. Billy thought this was a test of whether or not he was enlightened and remembering a Zen story about satori he burned a notebook in the lobby of Coca Cola and candy dispensers, walls painted army green, Maharishi notes curling like black fists on the table, and they opened the door suddenly rushing out with fire extinguishers and obviously he's passed the test they were so excited as the white mist covered his notes and put out the Zen blaze.

Then they let him sit on the floor inside while he played with a *Goldfinger* puzzle which an aid told him not to do but he continued and finally the big bear aid picked him up and carted him to the isolation cell, tossing him in and locking the door.

It was then that he alchemised the spirits as in the Pyramid of Gaza
A wink of good light to the left of my eye.

He took more Maharishi notes and scrawled obscenities over the Sanskrit, breaking the rules as a true mystic would and should, he got on all fours and howled like a wolf he bayed in the green chamber he let them enter him and turned them to ash as the beast bayed through his body.

> In Harlem's sweet sphinx room
> In Atlantic George's broom
> man o man
> Mick picked his own noise
> and ate the pranic prakritis
> twosome
> gruesome
> Buddha

They let him out of the cell in the morning. They didn't know he still carried a blue plastic space gun in his travel bag. The first thing he yelled was "Nyarlathotep!" (an H.P. Lovecraft devil-god), spotting the aged black man patient with long toenails jetting from his rubber sandals. The aides took the gun from his hand.

A psychiatrist interviewed him and he copied all the doctor's movements, shifting in his chair when the Doc shifted, looking to his left when Doc did, all the time watching out the window at each small figure passing, angel agents of good or the devil, all Shiva remember.

A friend came to see him and he said, "Jack, I can't take it anymore I want you to go out to your car," pointing through the chain link fence at the parking lot.

"What're you gonna do, Bill?"

"I'm leaving," and he climbed the fifteen-foot chainlink fence mad monkey. He quickly got to the other side and Jack disappeared into the building. Billy stood by the car, but Jack appeared with the psychiatrist.

"Come on back, Billy." The doctor held out his white starched arms. Billy felt judased. But he went back.

In two more days they decided he'd come down from all the effects of the LSD and released him to Jack's care, who drove him back to S.F., kind friend, since most of his friends had written him off as a drug head who'd bounce back into the ward over and over again. He even continued with the acid, found some in his pack he'd forgotten about, ranting to Jack over saucers that followed them in the fog up Highway One.

Still more acid, for school holiday wasn't up, throwing wine in his girlfriend's face and smashing the glass to the ground when she wouldn't believe he was the messiah.

The trips got uglier. He saw everyone as a demon on the streets. He finally stopped the acid as if a last spark of sanity deep in his brain knew that to pursue this any further would end in his death, or someone else's.

"Was it the divorce?" Dad said over the phone. Billy shrugged in San Francisco, the depressions so great now that when he came home from school he'd go straight to bed and try to sleep until morning, then going to the streetcar and wishing some crazed latino would put a random bullet in his brain the way the papers said it happened.

He went to the movies alone, but couldn't bare to watch *Dirty Little Billy*, a grim western on Billy the Kid, coming home and removing the slats from the stove and sticking his head inside, seeing what it might be like. And he burst into tears, wailing to Jesus, Krishna, Buddha, o so rudely fallen, once an incarnation, an avatar of the very deities he called to, now crumb boy, blast-heath of futility, loveless, so ugly to himself he expected a black insect to stare back at him from the mirror.

He saw a therapist, one the city provided. Six months later Billy stared out over the horizon as it purpled at six and wondered what had happened, was there any truth at all to what he had seen, now able to function and yet wondering, just wondering, who had he been as the Chemical Man?

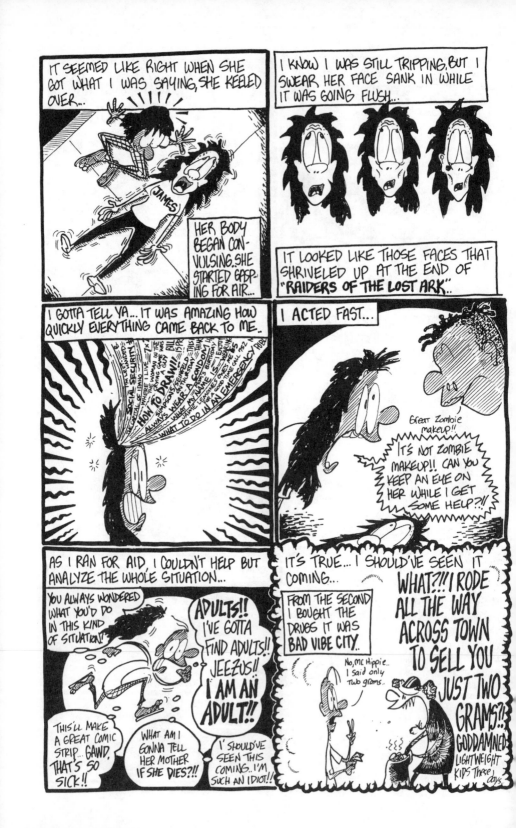

FAUNA URBANA part I
Stephen Fowler

Things were different back then. At that time our city was filled with pigeons: big gray birds with fat chests. Small nervous heads. Tiny red eyes. Most had a purplishgreen band of oil around their necks. And these pigeons were everywhere: every sidewalk, every alley, every rooftop, every park. They fed on garbage.

Then one April something happened. There was a weather system stalled over our city. The air was unusually warm and humid. Not enough wind to ruffle a feather. Each day the gray-green sky seemed to come a little closer.

The first hint I had that something was wrong came from my friend Tripolina. She lived in an attic apartment in a seedy part of town. Tripolina had complained for months about the pigeons nesting in the eaves of her house. Their scratching and cooing woke her every morning at dawn. But then one morning Tripolina overslept; the eaves were silent. A few more humid days passed, and a strong smell of decay started leaking into Tripolina's bedroom. Outside her window there was a steady buzzing of flies.

I offered to help. I leaned out her window and poked around under the eaves with a bent wire hanger. I snagged one dead pigeon, then another. The gray corpses fell to the sidewalk in a shower of feathers and dried birdshit. I managed to pull down two more bodies before the smell and the vertigo got to me.

Down on the sidewalk I examined the birds. Their eyes and beaks were full of maggots. I remember suspecting that Tripolina had poisoned them herself. She was that kind of girl.

At the time, I lived on an alley behind a sausage factory. Plenty of pigeons there. The next morning, as I walked to the subway station to catch the train to work, I spotted pigeon corpses: several on the sidewalk, one crushed in the street, and another limp on the hood of a parked car. This did seem strange to me, but not all that strange. It was early in the morning, before my first cup of coffee. With the eerie gray weather and my rush to get to work on time, I didn't reflect much on these dead tufts of feathers.

My suspicions weren't really aroused until after work that evening. On my way home from the train station I saw an old grocery cart approaching from the end of the alley. The cart was pushed by Alvaro: one of the neighborhood brats. Nine years old, backwards baseball cap, sweatshirt, basketball shoes. Alvaro was beaming. He shouted my name.

As he came nearer I noticed the wire basket of the cart was half-filled with dead pigeons: a hundred of them, maybe more. Alvaro's voice came out panting. "All the pigeons are dying. We're gonna have a bonfire in the vacant lot."

I looked at the cart and then at Alvaro. There was a damp hen-house smell in the air. I asked Alvaro how the birds had died.

"It's a pigeon-fever they get sick with. My dad he said it killed all the pigeons in Mexico last year. Now it's here. You can come and watch us burn them."

I turned down Alvaro's offer. I went home and washed my hands and changed my clothes. Then I took a shower and changed my clothes again. I figured: you can't be too clean during a pigeon epidemic.

At work the next morning I washed my hands every half-hour. But by midday I was starting to feel reckless. On my lunch break I decided to take a walk.

I counted twenty-six dead pigeons in two blocks. Apparently I was the only person who noticed them; the business people and window-shoppers on the sidewalks kept their eyes fixed straight ahead, like dignified men at a row of urinals. The only other person I saw looking at a pigeon corpse was an angry shopkeeper in a blue apron. He glared at the bird for a moment before sweeping it into the gutter with a pushbroom.

I walked on until I reached a small park: a landscaped square of concrete, surrounded by hotels and department stores. This park was renowned for its pigeon population. All the statues and benches were covered with white streaks of birdshit. Under the gray-green sky it was an eerie scene.

There were two kinds of pigeons in the park that day: sick ones and dead ones. Those still able to walk and fly did so uncertainly; their small eyes were filmy and their feathers were dirty and dishevelled. Many of the birds were confused. They turned their heads under their chests as if trying to see upside-down; they tripped over their own claws; or they performed flapping cartwheels as they tried to lift off from the ground. Some lay still, blinking at the sky. And many of them were simply dead: eyes whited over, claws splayed, wings limp.

In the midst of the pigeon carnage I noticed a man sitting by himself on a bench. A very old Chinese man, his scowling face as wrinkled as the brown paper bag in his lap.

As I approached him I realized why he was scowling. In a wide semi-circle at his feet he had scattered the ground with birdseed. But the pigeons were too sick to eat. They staggered through the seed blindly. One of them was having its death throes near the old man's feet. Its wings thrashed at the ground like an angry broom.

I watched for a moment, then felt a desire to talk to the man. "There's something wrong with the pigeons," I said.

The old man stared at me. He was silent. His expression was full of anger and suspicion.

I backed away from the man slowly, unsure of what I had done wrong. The birdseed crunched under my shoes. Then there was something soft and plump under my heel; my weight came down on a pigeon corpse. The worst of it was the sound. My foot squeezed a last lungful of air out of the bird with a wheezing gasp.

I hurried across the park, zig-zagging to avoid the sick pigeons that lay between me and the street. Ahead of me, a green truck had pulled up on the curb: Department of Public Works. The clean-up squad was already busy. A young man wearing an orange vest and a surgical mask was stabbing dead pigeons with a garbage skewer. The green plastic bag he carried was half full.

The next day—a Saturday—the rain started before dawn. The heavy vertical drops fell for two days without pause. I stayed in all weekend. When I emerged on Monday morning, I was in for a real treat.

Our city harbored more pigeons than any of us had ever imagined. The heavy rain dislodged thousands of previously unseen corpses. From rooftops, from gutters, from ornamental stonework and aluminum drainpipes, the oily gray bodies were washed down into the streets.

That morning after the rain, the weather was hot and hazy. On my walk to the train station I had to cross a flooded intersection: the dead pigeons had clogged the storm sewers. The street and part of the sidewalk had turned into an oily brown pond. There was a scum of garbage and feathers floating on its surface.

I can remember the relief I felt as I descended the escalator to the subway. It seemed that by leaving the street level, I was leaving the epidemic behind. This was an illusion. At the very foot of the escalator, a single pigeon corpse was being rolled over and over endlessly. Its body was nearly bald; it snagged on each step that went by beneath it. The escalator plucked the bird's feathers one pinch at a time.

The train carried me downtown. I stepped out of the station and into a cloud of flies. The heat and the moisture had started working on the dead pigeons. The streets were filled with a rich, nauseating odor. Men in ties hurried to their offices with handkerchiefs pressed over their mouths.

And me? I went to work. I went to work and washed my hands.

GHOST POEM
Bill Shields

I'm still losing parts of me in Vietnam
my brain dangles behind a dying body

I turn my head
& the bodies fall

I don't know why
these severe memories

of war keep me alone
& bloody in my boots

there is so much
I don't talk about

it kills me

THEY WANT YOU LIKE THAT
Joie Cook

there's always a crowd to destroy
yourself in
george told me: they want you like
that: worn, drunk, depreciated,
mumbling to concrete in search
of a bottle or one last handout
they want you like that:
breathing fire into someone
else's lust but all alone;
put on remote control
by other peoples' saviors
they want you like that!
hurting in napa with a tube
up your ass,
jaundiced eyes and green teeth
they want you like that!
burned out at thirty
buried at forty
crying tears that no one sees
'til the pallbearers
put the final dust
in the dampness:

cold/flesh/ZERO.

WHO IS LUCKY?
Dan Archibald

i was watching the 4:00 news
& saw all these folks
coming off a wrecked plane
crying
moaning
pissing about the narrow escape
which everyone survived
No casualties.
The majority were shaking
speaking of the horrors
all but one
a Mexican immigrant
waiting for his luggage
burn-bandaged arm
He alone seemed to know
the bills
the jobs
the hard times all waiting
in the mailbox
he, wanting to get on w/the damn ride
no one else would ever see.

WALKING TO MASAYA
NICARAGUA, JULY 1986
Dashka Slater

The vast field behind the bus station was filled with people by the time we got there. Sue and I had been worried they would have already left and we would have missed the Repliegue but this was based on a misplaced sense of punctuality. Waiting was part of the ritual.

Walking into that crowd was like walking into the sea. It stretched everywhere in all directions and suddenly we were just salty drops in the jumble of it. The sea was made up of young people mostly, the majority in uniform. The youngest ones were about fourteen years old.

I looked around. Up above the endless plain of heads and olive-green shoulders, towers were being formed. Three men stood in a tight circle while three others climbed onto their shoulders. Then a third group was lifted up to stand on the shoulders of the second rung. These narrow pillars would waver for a moment and then those at the top jumped backwards, landing in the arms of their comrades as the whole structure toppled. As I stood with my friend watching the towers rising and falling, I was grabbed by a bunch of young men who had come running through the mass. They laid me on a net of their arms and shouted, "Uno! Dos! Tres!" before tossing me up into the thick twilight.

Flung into the sky, I looked around to see dozens of bodies floating in the air above the crowd. We flew upwards with our chests leading the way and our arms thrown out in surprise. Then gravity sucked me down again and the green sea rose up to wash over me. When the boys put me on the ground I felt like kissing their stubbly cheeks but they were off again to grab another girl and send her flying.

Ortega spoke for a long time. I stood on tiptoes to watch him. His words drifted over the field, propelled by two loudspeakers mounted on scaffolding. Boys hung from the scaffolding and shouted out jokes to him. He answered back, joking but also very serious. I thought he was one of the most serious men I had ever seen. Still the words came like a steady rain over that green, green sea.

We walked along a dirt road through the forest. It was night when we finally left the field to begin the walk to Masaya. The young soldiers took off practically running, pushing past each other to get ahead. They were drinking rum out of pocket flasks, tripping over tree roots, calling out to each other, singing. Tossed about in what was now a river I thought about the thirty kilometers ahead. Had the army trained these people so well that they could skip through this all night march? Sue was getting lost in the current. She and I linked hands to keep from being separated.

We walked on and on through the dark and the woods. What was this march about anyway? All day people had been asking us if we meant to do it, but no one had explained exactly what it was. So now we were walking along the rutted road with the trees thick above us, blocking out the sky. There was no moon. My eyes fixed on the tall grass by the roadside. I thought about sleeping in it, about waking up in the dewy grass with a grey light coming down on the woods.

The man who slowed to join us was named Martin. He was older than most of the crowd, in his early thirties. He told us he had walked the Repliegue that first time, during the last year of Somoza, and had walked it every year since. Tell us the story, we asked.

One month before the Triumph, Somoza's national guard planned to attack a barrio in Managua that Somoza considered a revolutionary pocket. The night before the attack was to occur, the entire neighborhood, whole families, evacuated the barrio and walked all night until they reached Masaya, a liberated town thirty kilometers away. Every year since then this famous retreat, the *repliegue*, has been reenacted.

I imagined the walk on that night, unlit, quiet, the dirt scuffed up by children's careless feet.

Now it was a little lighter and houses began to appear on the sides of the road. Wires were strung between tree trunks and festooned with FSLN banners. The people who lived in the houses had set up chairs on the side of the road and some were offering pots of stew and some were selling soda pop. Martin bought us sodas and an old man who had been sitting in one of the chairs got up and insisted I sit in it. Another chair was vacated and offered to my friend. We sat like dusty princesses while the old man and several of his family gathered round to beam at us.

"Not much longer," Martin kept telling me. The road became paved and we walked up a steep hill. The tanks that had been slowed by the crush of people on the dirt road could pull ahead now. "Look," Martin said and pointed down to a city that lay below us. "Masaya."

I didn't expect the long expanse of pasture nor the endless outskirts of town populated by little bars and wooden houses.

"We're almost there," Martin told us, but it took us an hour to walk from the edge of town to the center.

We came at last to cobblestones and stone buildings. Soldiers lay sleeping in the streets. We threaded among these puddles of olive drab that grew wider as we neared the main plaza.

In the park, people were sleeping everywhere, on the paths, in the grass, under bushes. We found a little spot in the grass just as it began to rain. I wrapped myself in my poncho and curled up, listening to the marimba that drifted from the nearby hall and the sound of the fat raindrops landing on my plastic shell.

When I woke, Martin and Sue were kissing. When I woke again, Martin was gone and the rain had turned our bedding into mud.

ENLIGHTENMENT AND
MUSCULAR DYSTROPHY
Eli Coppola

The first miles were easy,
you've heard it before.
I took sixteen years in giant strides,
on impulse, in flight.
Breath-less, care-less
child.
And it was over about that quickly.

I was left with a string of small water planets,
a charmed circle I wear around my throat.
It's taken me these last fourteen years to learn that certain things
broken
stay broken.
And also to notice the space the breaking has made
that lets the whole world in.

Now wherever I go I always go slowly.
Gravity and I have long conversations through my legs.
I cooperate with the smallest pebble.
I study imperceptible inclines
I fall and I   get up and I fall and   I get
up   and   I fall and   I   get up.
My miles are good long miles.

When I work hard I think better.
But I lose a little more each year,
a few degrees of motor control.
So far always
less than they predict,
and always more
than I can surrender.

This year, in a photograph, I did not recognize my hands.
It's a fierce thing, this enlightenment.

Claudia

BY DEBBIE DRECHSLER © 1 9 9 3

THERE WAS THIS GIRL AT MY SCHOOL...

HI CLAUDIA!

WHO WAS THE SHYEST PERSON I EVER MET!

UMM...UHH...OH...MM...

SHE WOULD PRACTICALLY HAVE A CORONARY JUST FROM TRYING TO SAY HELLO...

OH...UHH...WELL...UMM...HI.

BUT IF SHE GOT CALLED ON IN CLASS, SHE WAS COMPLETELY NORMAL.

...AND YOU ALSO HAVE TO CONSIDER THE RELATIVE WEIGHTS OF THE TWO OBJECTS...

IN SCIENCE I GOT ASSIGNED CLAUDIA FOR MY PROJECT PARTNER. AT FIRST, I WONDERED HOW WE WOULD DO IT WITHOUT TALKING...

BUT, I FOUND OUT, AS LONG AS I DIDN'T GET PERSONAL, EVERYTHING WOULD BE ALRIGHT.

WELL, WE COULD MAKE A BIG POSTER OF IT. I CAN DRAW PRETTY GOOD.

THAT'S A GOOD IDEA!

I ALSO FOUND OUT SHE WAS ABOUT THE SMARTEST PERSON I EVER MET.

...SO WE CAN PUT IN SOME DECIDUOUS TREES, AND SOME CONIFERS. ALSO, THE ANIMALS THAT LIVE IN THE DIFFERENT HABITATS,

SINCE CLAUDIA HAD NO TALENT FOR ART, SHE DECIDED TO DO ALL THE WRITING ON OUR PROJECT.

...AND YOU DO ALL THE PICTURES, I THINK THAT'S FAIR, DON'T YOU?

YEAH, I GUESS.

SHE GOT AWFUL PICKY ABOUT THE FACTS.

THIS CAN'T BE RIGHT! THIS LEAF DOESN'T LOOK LIKE THAT IN REAL LIFE!

SHE TRIED TO DRAW IT FOR ME.

OH! I WISH I COULD DRAW!

ME TOO! I CAN'T SEE THE DIFF!

I DIDN'T SEE WHY WE COULDN'T LET IT GO.

WHO'LL KNOW THE DIFFERENCE ANYWAY?

ME! AND IT'LL DRIVE ME NUTS!!

ON SATURDAY, WE MET AT THE OLD RAILROAD BED SO SHE COULD SHOW ME SOME OF THOSE LEAVES FOR OUR PROJECT.

DOUBLE DIP
Nancy Depper

this morning I stared
at my hand
solid as an egg, with all
the softness womanhood evokes
these fingers
lined up like kisses
in a row
pulling out the tangles
rubbing lotions, blending
powders of color for the lips
all the daily intimacies
raising my hand, bringing it
down again

I did not choose a lover
last night, nor will I
tonight, perhaps, but
the work of the body
the body of work is no one else's chore
my task my hand
lacing boot ties, dressing
warmly, choosing the stillness
of my pocket or
cold fingering of the bus pass
I am still decorated with the ring
that the vendor thought
she'd sell to a child
but it fit me, a quiet shine
of support for the first knuckle

this morning my hand
lay still as a painting
not worried
(the palm line runs
like needlepoint down a long leg)
but not moving either
I lace with my teeth
let my elbows go dry
I am still no one's chore
raising my hand, bringing it
down again

DOES THE CAT APPROVE OF THIS?
Michele C.

The buzzer rang and he pushed open the wrought-iron security gate, then a few feet beyond that, the door into the building. The entryway was a small square just large enough to allow for the swing of the door. The first leg of the narrow stairway immediately and steeply ascended, two sagging flights to each floor of apartments. She lived on the fourth. As he trudged his way toward her abode he imagined their meeting with the objective sensibility of one whose curiosity will be satisfied regardless of his degree of anticipation.

She was the type of cat owner who required any potential friend or suitor to appear subjugated to her pet. Though the idea of sucking up to a cat like a potential stepchild was sickening, it actually paid to be on the cat's good side. It seemed that whenever a visitor of whom the cat disapproved was in the pad, the animal would wait until the unfavorable human was engrossed in conversation or busy some other way and then it would shit, piss or spray on some personal possession: book, coat, purse or hat, anything that belonged to that person and was not in immediate view. Imagine the surprise of finding an expression of this cat's displeasure! He had heard all about it from a guy on whose leather jacket collar the cat had deposited a remarkably soft and fragrant mound. Of course, she subscribed to the theory that pets, and cats especially, do not know why they are being punished unless they are caught in the act and disciplined on the spot, as it were. To most it didn't matter anyway; even the most severe cat beating was no consolation for a moist turd in a shoe or a notebook sprayed with skanky musk.

He reminded himself to keep all his belongings together by his side until they left for dinner. He rang the second bell outside the door marked number twelve. He waited. He wondered what was taking so long, it wasn't as if she didn't know he was on his way up. He heard the deadbolt turn and she finally opened the door just wide enough to fit her face between it and the frame as she shoved Marble-Eyes, the infamous feline, back with one foot. When she saw he was indeed her expected guest, she scooped the cat up and perched it on her shoulder as she admitted him to the cluttered apartment.

She was a dabbling sort of gal—dabbled in pop psychology and compulsive shopping and a certain dance style she had perfected in the three by four and a half square feet of open space in the center of her teenage bedroom at her mother's house. Piles of books were stacked on top of overflowing crates of books. Many more were unread than read. It was difficult to find time to read when she was so busy shopping for more books and other collectable objects. The rooms were soaked with latte talk of cafe adventures and other alternative lifestyle activities. She had hip music on the stereo; her record collection ran like a college radio station playlist. Dubious art made a collage of her walls and tables. Things, things, and more things! He sat in one of those rust-tone iron butterfly chairs covered with a fuchsia canvas sling, the kind that used to be suburban patio furniture but had somehow become integrated into the apartments of urban-dwelling gals.

As they talked, windchimes clanged and the cat made several approaches, whether toward him in friendship or toward his coat in treachery, he could not say. He extended his hand a couple of times attempting to pet it but the cat either stepped back, lip aloofly curled, or reeled in terror as if it expected to be hit. It instilled a distinct sense of guilt in him although he had done nothing. He wondered if she would assume him to be one of those people toward whom animals are instinctively wary and what effect that would have on her estimation of him.

She poured him another glass of cheap red wine and like a warm and soothing garnet blush, it spread peace through his body as he swallowed. He soon decided he didn't give a shit about some asinine cat's impact on his potential love/sex life. He took out a joint which they smoked as she talked. Words fell from her mouth like the endless tiny bubbles of a froth, thick, puddled around the feet of the listener, everything she said swaying with the illusion of water. Her chatter moved in waves against his ears, ceaseless digressions pulled along by intricate links of connection. He began to wonder what he was doing, listening to her blather about subjects that held no interest for him. Why was he there at all? He looked at her short blonde hair, dark at the roots, her carefully lined eyes squinting through cigarette smoke and below, her greased pink mouth opening and shutting, opening and shutting as she talked.

Maybe he was just stoned, but it seemed to him he had reached some meditative plateau of Zen insight while locked in the vacuum of her incessant talk that was like a wall of white noise, and to which he need not pay attention. His isolated mind was full of questions he suddenly had time to answer while her monomaniacal ravings held him as if gagged. Why, Why, WHY echoed in his head and he realized he had no good answer. He realized also that he did not want to spend another minute with this woman.

He could not remember what about her had attracted and convinced him he wanted to date her. Why he had imagined he might enjoy sex with her was a mystery as well. He stood abruptly, and incidentally on the paw of the skulking Marble-Eyes who had been carefully sniffing the armpits of his coat. As the cat screeched in pain he ground his heel down a little harder and pivoted as he snatched up his possessions. He left the apartment without saying goodbye. When she was alone and the record stopped, the room was finally silent.

LAUNDROMAT
Ann Peters

Sunday afternoon, I did my wash
on First Ave. and 'F' street, all loads in
and I, sitting, calmly reading Colette when
the drunk fell through the window.

Everything shattered and splashed,
briefly schizoid then blood ripe from
a tube,
strung along on that high cable forming
around the piss marks on his light blue trousers.

The joy of this single intrusion, real, in fine form
in water form. All reactions were fluid.
His laundry companion was furious, in
soaked blue jeans.
Goddamn shit. That's what he said.

After the blood and glass,
the suturing of the gash,
the imminent threat of gangrene and he,
with a swollen water arm,
after that everyone bent along the same,
doing wash with January breathing in.

ASSAULT WITH A DEADLY STORY
Robert Howington

I used to edit and publish a little magazine, *A Bug in My Fries*, and one time a guy from New York City, Steven Munden, sent me some of his stuff, a mishmash of strange and incompetent short stories and bad poetry, and a cover letter that contained not only his best story but his best writing as well. In the letter, he wrote that he had been in prison for robbery and aggravated assault, but that the cops had never caught him for worse crimes he'd done, like rapes and murders.

"I think I've killed maybe at least five people," he wrote in terrible, childlike scribbles. "Maybe more because I'm drunk and high a lot and I black out on a regular basis so I don't know really what all I've done. I'm kinda like a werewolf I guess. I change and become something terrible. I slash and pound and after a while blood is all over my clothes and I walk home. Cops see me but they don't stop. To them I'm just another guy with blood all over him. I do work but I'm quiet and keep by myself and nobody seems interested in me. I have to be careful. I do talk when I'm drunk and one guy I killed I had to kill him because I told him all about how I raped this woman, giving every detail, and he tells me this woman with the red hair and blue eyes sounds a lot like his sister who had got raped. I told him the woman said her name was Sandra and he jumped me. I pulled a knife and I woke up in a gutter and walked home. Killing people is not so hard. If you get mad enough, it's easy."

I liked his letter so much I printed it. Soon after mailing out the issue in which the letter appeared a cop from New York called and asked if I would send him the original via overnight express. He told me they had Munden in custody and were going to charge him with murder one.

"His letter you printed was read here in New York by some people who saw the magazine at an out-of-the-way bookstore."

"That would be See Hear," I interrupted. "I always send them a few copies of each issue."

"Yeah, well, they alerted us and we contacted the woman he talked about raping. We found out who she was by taking the clues he gave in the letter, her hair color, eye color and first name, and punched those into a computer. She came up almost immediately and her case was still open.

"We called her and sure enough her brother had been killed in a bar fight. She ID'd your writer and we got a warrant for his arrest and picked him up at his job. He's admitted to the brother's murder and had hinted at one more. After we interrogate him further I'm sure he'll come clean with everything he's done. He's starting to like the limelight, with the attention and the reporters and all."

I sent the cop the letter and a few months later I learned from a *New York Post* reporter who called me that Munden had been found guilty and sentenced to life in prison for raping and murdering a mother of two.

"Your friend used a serving spoon on her," the reporter said. "He's a twisted sick motherfucker. He has the eyes of a crazed pit bull and very pale skin. He laughed out loud at the trial all the time for no reason we could detect. He seems to have a lot going on inside his head and it apparently has to come out somehow. The DA figured this murdered mother case would be easier to prosecute than the murder of the brother of the rape victim. Your friend has admitted to three other killings too, a prostitute in an alley, an old man in a park, and get this, a dog in a neighbor's backyard. Since he doesn't want to appeal this first case, and he didn't want to because he hated sitting all day in cold courtrooms, they won't go forward with the other cases. They'll certainly never let this guy out on parole. Besides, he says he likes it on the inside. It gives him time to write he says."

"That would account for all these stories and poems he sends me," I said. "They're all so pitifully bad. I tell him they suck but he keeps sending them to me. He's thinking about switching to screenplays and I sent him a book, *Successful Scriptwriting*, to read and study. But his letters are incredible, they ramble on forever and he talks about shit that he's done and it's truly maddening. I plan on printing these letters in my next issue."

I told him that Munden had impressed me with one letter by quoting a line from a Charles Bukowski short story called *Decline and Fall*. It read, *...somehow you get to thinking a murdered thing should keep screaming.* "Bukowski might know about drinking and women and fucking," he wrote in his scrawl, "but he don't know killing. When you done with them they lay there and they are dead and there is no way for them to scream because they are dead and everything stops. Bukowski will know when he kills somebody how it is really."

I told the reporter I'd forward him a copy of the next issue. After putting the receiver down, I walked out to my mailbox and looked inside it. There in an envelope, marked with an address that said it came from a New York State Penitentiary, was some more wisdom from Steven Munden. I ripped it open and read what he had to say right there on the sidewalk.

CASE STUDY
Alice Olds-Ellingson

Surreal,
I've led
a different
life, kicked
around & fucked
over but I
had the
beauty
all
the
time
I'm not selfish
it was always
magic
like the
strange dawn
at 3 in the
afternoon
I get you
to KNOW what I mean
like another memory
like snap doo-AH
with a girl's jazz
band I was the

only audience
harmony. It was close.
The owner of the gig
kept coming
in like the
coda
wanting me to shut up
didn't listen to what
I added to the sex
of an all-woman sex band
he was only male after all
not a peacock
male
how could
he know

THE ONLY THING THAT'S KEEPING HIM SANE
Jon Longhi

It was a Wednesday night at 2:30 in the morning and I was contentedly snoozing away in my bed when my neighbors who live directly above my bedroom came home and began having a party. They put on melody destroying industrial music, turned the stereo up to level ten and began dancing in their combat boots. I woke up screaming from a dream of hippos, terrified in my grogged-out state that war had been declared on Haight Street. When I realized it was just a party I put on my sweat pants and Dingo boots and went outside where I began banging on their front door. For fifteen minutes I knocked, but they were making so much noise they couldn't hear me. Their buzzer was broken. So I went back to bed.

After two more hours of staring at my ceiling through a nonstop medley of feedback white noise, I got up and called the police. The dispatcher could hardly hear what I was saying because the upstairs stereo was booming through the floor with a squealing vocal about killing every white child. Of course the cops never came. So I lay staring at the ceiling, wide awake, listening to buzzsaw percussion tracks and the stomping of combat boots until 9:30 in the morning. I got up at quarter till seven and called the police again, but they still must have been busy buying donuts or something, and never showed up. When the last of the partygoers passed out at 9:30 I thought, 'Finally. Now I can get some sleep.' My alarm went off at 9:45.

When I got to work an hour later it was the busiest day of the Christmas season. I spent the whole shift sweating my ass off on the phone, talking to three customers at once, drinking endless cups of coffee just to keep my metabolism lit. By the time I got off at seven I was shot. There wasn't a drop of adrenaline left in me.

I left the office and dutifully locked myself out of the building. It wasn't until after I closed the door behind me that I realized I had left my glasses and my work keys inside. I pulled at the door handle but it was bolted solid. Fuck it, I'd have to make it home without them.

I walked over to the mailbox and began to unlock my moped. While I was fiddling with my keys someone approached through the periphery of my vision. When I look up it's this big yahoo dude who weighs about 250 pounds and, with the exception of his beer gut, most of it's hardass muscle.

"Look, man," he says to me. "I've written to my congressman but he won't listen to me. I mean they've announced it on CNN and all but still no one believes it!"

"What?" I asked, not wanting to offend him.

"Angel Dust is the cure for AIDS!"

Oh no.

"It kills the virus!" he screamed. "It kills all diseases. Why won't the government listen?!"

I hurriedly went back to unlocking my bike.

"They should prescribe Angel Dust to everyone. Every American citizen! This!" he shouted, holding out a joint of dust in his hand. "Is the wonder drug of the '90s!"

By this time I had the bike unlocked and was trying to kick start it. But it just wouldn't fire up. So I kept pulling at the clutch and kicking at the starter.

"Angel Dust is the only thing that's kept me healthy," he screamed. "It's protected me. I would have been dead a long time ago if it weren't for this stuff. But why don't they put a story about me on the news? Huh? Why doesn't Dan Rather tell the American people that this stuff is better than penicillin? Why! Why?!" He began shaking me.

"I don't know! I don't know!" I managed to jiggle out. "I mean,

AZT doesn't seem to be doing too good a job."

I just wanted to agree with him if that was possible. The guy was so excited that he kept spitting in my face as he screamed. And the whole time my bike won't start. I keep kicking at the pedal but the engine just won't turn over, I can't even get a sputter or cough out of the plugs, the whole scene was like a fucking horror movie, all it needed was a scary sound track. Every business along the street was closed for the night with their security fences down and all the lights out. The whole damn street was dark, shadowy, and deserted.

"I mean people don't even need to eat if they do Angel Dust," he kept shaking the joint in my face, spitting all over me. "But the government won't tell anyone. They want everyone to die! It's driving me out of my mind. But I'm fucking lucky to have found this stuff. I don't know where I'd be without it. I mean, Angel Dust is the only thing that's keeping me sane!"

At that point I said, "Excuse me, I have to push start this bike." And I took off pushing the moped down the street. I ran with the bike for four or five blocks and it still wouldn't start, but at least I was away from the Dust guy. Finally I pulled the bike up onto the sidewalk and kept trying to get it to turn over. For almost fifteen minutes I kept popping the clutch and then who should come walking by but, yes, you guessed it. He ran right up to me and began yelling, "Look, man, I've written to my congressman but he won't listen to me. I mean they've announced it on CNN and all but..." and he went into an exact repeat of his Angel Dust as Messiah monologue. After awhile I just looked up at him with a sour expression and he stopped. "Oh, it's you," he said with a deflated tone, and at that he walked off in search of other converts.

A couple minutes later I got the bike started and from the rattle of the engine I knew the problem was that it needed oil. I drove to the nearest auto parts store and bought a quart of two-stroke. I was so exhausted and shaky that I poured half the quart all over the front of me. By the time I got home it had soaked down to my underwear. In my room, I stripped off my clothes and realized there was not one iota of strength left in me. I had to sleep. Immediately. It was a miracle I had even been able to stand that long. The sheets beckoned. As soon as I laid down on the bed I heard the door to the upstairs apartment bang open. Twenty or thirty combat-booted feet clomped in like thunder, samples of feedback and car crashes blared out of the neighbors' stereo speakers so loudly they may as well have been in my own room, and I realized I wouldn't have any peace for at least another eight hours.

DO YOU REALIZE THAT SLEEP ACCOUNTS FOR ONE-THIRD OF THE AVERAGE PERSON'S LIFE? *ONE-THIRD* OF OUR *ENTIRE* EXISTENCE (AS WE KNOW IT) DOWN THE TUBES... SQUANDERED... *GONE!* READ ON, AND I THINK YOU'LL AGREE...

SLEEP=WASTE

©1994 by ADRIAN TOMINE

WITH ONLY ABOUT FIFTEEN HOURS OF CONSCIOUSNESS IN EACH DAY, ONLY SO MUCH CAN BE ACCOMPLISHED. AS A RESULT, THE THINGS I REALLY CARE ABOUT HAVE OFTEN TAKEN A BACK SEAT TO THE MORE *DREARY* ASPECTS OF LIFE, SUCH AS SCHOOL, WORK, MINDLESS ERRANDS, ETC.

WHY? WHY?

MATH TEST
NO CALCULATORS!

IF I DIDN'T HAVE TO SLEEP, I COULD ACCOMPLISH THOSE THINGS AND STILL HAVE AMPLE TIME FOR MORE PRODUCTIVE, ENRICHING ACTIVITIES...

LIKE DRAWING COMICS!

BUT ADRIAN— YOU'RE OVERLOOKING ONE IMPORTANT FACT!

EH?

SLEEP *FEELS* GOOD!

FEELS GOOD?!! LYING IDLY FOR HOURS ON END *FEELS GOOD?* I'LL TELL YOU WHAT *FEELS GOOD*... INKING A SATISFYING PAGE OF COMICS *FEELS GOOD!* READING A GOOD BOOK *FEELS GOOD!* SPENDING TIME WITH THE ONE YOU LOVE *FEELS GOOD!*

OKAY, YOU LAZY DIM-WIT?

MR. HIGH-STRUNG

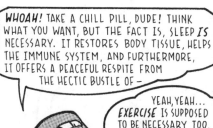

SINCE IT SEEMS THAT MANY CONFLICTS ARISE SIMPLY FROM PEOPLE'S CONSTANT INTERACTION AND CONTACT WITH EACH OTHER, VIOLENCE AND UNHAPPINESS WOULD ABOUND!

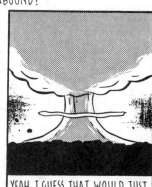

SO IDEALLY, *I'D* BE THE ONLY ONE WHO DIDN'T HAVE TO SLEEP...

ADRIAN, YOU PUT OUT AN ISSUE OF OPTIC NERVE EVERY OTHER MONTH, GO TO SCHOOL, WORK, AND STILL HAVE TIME TO MAINTAIN FRIENDSHIPS AND RELATIONSHIPS! WHAT'S YOUR SECRET?

ORGANIZATION AND DEDICATION, I GUESS.

IN MY RESEARCH, I HAVE COME ACROSS A FEW HEROIC PIONEERS WHO TRIED TO OVERCOME THE TEMPTATION OF SLEEP. SUCH AS *RANDY GARDNER*, A 17-YEAR-OLD WHO STAYED AWAKE FOR *11* DAYS STRAIGHT!

HE EMPLOYED A TECHNIQUE CALLED "MICRO-SLEEP," IN WHICH HE WOULD MENTALLY CONCENTRATE ALL THE REST HE NEEDED INTO ONE MOMENT, AND THEN NOD OFF FOR LESS THAN A SECOND!

AH...THAT FELT *GREAT!* GOOD MORNING!

WHEN HE FINALLY FELL ASLEEP, HE AWOKE ONLY 15 HOURS LATER, FEELING FINE!

HMM...BUT ALL HE DID FOR THOSE 11 DAYS WAS SIT AROUND AND PLAY PINBALL...

NEVERTHELESS, HE IS STILL AN INSPIRING INDIVIDUAL... AS IS *MAUREEN WESTON*, A WOMAN FROM ENGLAND WHO BROKE ALL RECORDS BY STAYING AWAKE FOR *18* CONSECUTIVE DAYS!

OF COURSE, ALL *SHE* DID WAS SIT IN A ROCKING CHAIR ... PLUS, SHE EVENTUALLY BEGAN TO EXPERIENCE *HALLUCINATIONS*...

I ACCOMPLISH MORE IN A NORMAL DAY THAN THESE PEOPLE DID IN OVER A WEEK! SO MUCH FOR THE "COLD TURKEY" METHOD...

RECENTLY, I THOUGHT I'D STRUCK UPON THE PERFECT SOLUTION... I WOULD SLOWLY **WEAN** MYSELF OFF OF SLEEP, SETTING MY ALARM 10 MINUTES EARLIER EACH DAY.

BRILLIANT! THE CHANGE WILL BE SO GRADUAL, MY BODY WON'T EVEN NOTICE!

BUT ALAS, MY EXPERIMENT WAS A FAILURE: WITHIN TWO WEEKS, I WAS SICK AND EXHAUSTED!

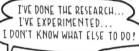

I'VE DONE THE RESEARCH... I'VE EXPERIMENTED... I DON'T KNOW WHAT ELSE TO DO!

RIGHT HERE, BUDDY! Y'KNOW WHAT THIS IS, DUDE? IT'S **SPEED**, Y'DIG? A FEW LINES OF THIS SHIT AND YOU'LL BE UP FOR **DAYS**, BRO'!

DON'T YOU UNDERSTAND? I'M LOOKING FOR A **CURE**... NOT JUST TEMPORARY RELIEF! AS SOON AS THAT WORE OFF, I'D GO STRAIGHT TO SLEEP! FURTHERMORE, WHAT YOU'RE OFFERING ME IS AN ADDICTIVE, PARANOIA-INDUCING **DRUG**... HARDLY A SOLUTION TO THE QUANDARY AT HAND!

GO BACK TO L.A., YOU FUCKIN' **DRUGGIE!**

SO, UNTIL SOMEONE MAKES SOME **BREAK-THROUGH**, I'LL HAVE TO RESIGN MYSELF TO THE FACT THAT WITHOUT 7 HOURS OF SLEEP AND AT LEAST 3 CUPS OF COFFEE PER DAY, I'M WORTHLESS!

SIGH

IN FACT, ALL THIS TALKING HAS REALLY TIRED ME OUT!

I'M...HELPLESS...

WHAT A CURSE!

Z Z Z

GOOD-NIGHT!

sleep = waste • 209

MEMORIES
Jerry D. Miley

I remember memories of awakening
with no memories:
I remember trying to forget:
never do I remember such hopeless
longing to stand up and do something
as in a skid row hotel room.
Two years covered up in cold
sheet warmth windows closed,
even the noise was cold,
and steam hissing like a snake
biting itself to sleep by mid-morning,
rattling dreams tossed
themselves a hot plate,
plugging in heat like a stopped-up sink
giving off floor water
when you turned it on:
plaster cracking
sound of ancient pipe.
I am moving out of that hotel
to this day,
my overlarge heavy white coat
with no buttons
is on my back by 9:30,
and I am waiting forever to go
back to sleep,
because I cannot bear to stay awake
and this is human life
when I am waiting
not to be hungry.

CHELSEA HOTEL
(HARRY'S STORY)
Kimi Sugioka

Got a letter today from an old friend of mine. For twelve years we
got drunk and broke a lot of bottles together. Penny's sort of an occult-
artist-leader. I didn't hear from her for a long time 'cause she was mad at
me. You see I had this friend, Joe, who accidentally murdered this other
guy. I'm sure it was an accident. But this friend of mine, Dan Whistler,
he came into my room at the Chelsea Hotel, grinning and yelling, "Billy
Maybeck's dead!" But he wasn't the one who murdered him. You see
Dan was Jenny Whistler's husband and she was having an affair with Billy
Maybeck. But it was my friend Joe who probably committed the murder.
Someone else found the body all trussed up and told the hotel manager.
He tried to make it to look like a natural death because he didn't want
the police coming around.

Well, this other guy was going to jail for three thirty-year sentences,
so he said he'd take the rap. That was nice of him. He came from a whole
family of criminals you know and the grandmother was the worst! She
raised all these people who had a one-word vocabulary of "Yeah."
Anyway, he went to jail for it instead of Joe.

Well, Penny had a big mouth, you know, it wasn't all just lipstick.
She got to talking big, angry at my friend who may have committed the
murder. I'm not really sure.

She sent me this postcard one time and I put a big X on the address and wrote 'Address Unknown' and I never heard from her again — till today. She said she'd send me money if she knew the right address. She knows I always need money.

So I called her up and she said she could hardly get out of bed anymore, except occasionally, when she uses her walker. Here I am calling her, and she can't get out of bed, and I can hardly walk.

A REFLECTION
Bruce Jackson

He thought the rain was falling hardest where he was. The abused and broken buildings were surely sucking water from the sky. Puddles grew beneath his feet waiting for the rainfall, with the touch of the rainfall they would jump away from the ground, away from the alley, each shot an escape. The puddles beneath his feet would jump, get high, but as quickly as they'd rise, they'd fall back into the brokenness, back into the alley to wait for their next jump. He wondered if there was pain in their waiting. He wondered in pain, waiting.

The rain fell, harder now and more intensely. Things that before were clearly visible vanished with the fall. The brilliant light of the used car lot at the end of the alley became a blur, a shadow through the translucent wall of water that fell to the alley from the sky. Because of the rain, the alley darkened, and parts once lighted by the lot fell victim to the rain, to its shadow. The Italian restaurant three buildings back became a victim. He stood in the five step pit that led to the back door of the restaurant. The pit was flooded to the first step, but he stood, partially sheltered from the rain by the break of the door. A black trench coat covered most of his body, and although it was soaked, he was dry all the way down to his ankles. He trembled, not from the cold of the rainfall but from the pain of his dryness, his waiting.

His head dropped. His eyes closed, and for a very small part of a second, he slept. For the remaining part of that second, he was slapped to awakeness. Pain ripped through his inside. He jerked as if he could avoid it, but he couldn't. He tightened his muscles and waited for it to dull. It bent him over, but soon he could stand straight again. He concentrated on standing straight, and the pain became acceptable. As soon as he could think again, he stood on his tiptoes, looked down the alley, the other way. No one was there. No one was coming, goddamit.

The rain slowed. Puddles grew, but there was only waiting. Nothing could escape the ground. The rain fell from the clouds but lacked the power to give freedom from the alley. He looked down at the pit. His eyes had adjusted to the dark but he could see nothing beneath him. He could only feel the water as it drained into the five-holed circle at the center of the broken, black cement floor. When he could no longer feel the water, he stepped into the center of the pit and looked down the alley. The used car lot had a revolving sign. *Lucky Jim's* was on one side. On the other was the time.

He spoke in a whisper, "8:31," still afraid to break his concentration. "Where is he?"

For a second he was terrified that the rain had delayed or stopped his smack. He could not allow that thought to last, so he laughed and told himself, "He'll be here any minute. The motherfucker's just late."

He stood on his tiptoes, looked again, no one. He stepped back into the break of the door, looked up at the stairs in front of him. When he was certain that he could be seen, he tried to calm himself down. He rocked his body, flexed his arms, scratched his veins. "It's gonna be cool. It's gonna be cool," he said. "He's coming. It's gonna be cool."

He shook the rain off his coat and stood, waiting...

Lightning!

He glanced up and it was gone. When he looked down, the pain caught his vacant mind. It ripped through him slowly, much dryer than he'd ever imagined possible. He gritted his teeth tightly until it seemed his upper and lower jaw were one thing. He closed his eyes hard and squeezed a tear from the corner. The pain dulled, but now he was afraid of it. He had to think of something quickly. He had to occupy his mind, so he remembered that the first drop of rain had fallen on him that day. He remembered that the fall had ended on his hand, that the waiting was over for the first drop of rain. There would be no escapes. He remembered glancing at the clock at the end of the alley when that drop hit his hand, 7:50. He remembered walking down into the five-step pit of the Italian restaurant, "Shit, it's gonna rain."

But it was raining now. It was 8:33. He was waiting. He didn't want to remember anymore. He got nervous, terrified, and in a voice that was only half a whisper, he cried, "Where the fuck is he?"

He stomped up the steps, looked, no one, then the pain. He eased back into the pit, wrapped his arms around his stomach and cried, "Where the fuck is he? Where the fuck is he?"

He reached into his pocket, pulled out a neatly folded roll of bills. It was wet, but the smack wouldn't care. The rain hadn't done any serious damage. Six twenties, a ten, a five, and two ones, all the money was still there. He jammed the roll deeply into his pocket, gripping the bills tightly in his hand. The money had to be there. He'd worked too hard that day. When he thought of his work, he felt a slickness on the bills in his hand. When he realized it wasn't water, he tried to think of nothing, but then there was pain, then a thought erupted, a memory erupted.

He was at the northwestern station, hidden in the shadows, behind the broken soda machine where he'd spent most of the day. His black trench coat made him almost invisible, and as the people passed, he observed freely, waiting for a moment. Empty, cold, he did not feel. There was only pain to feel, to remind him. His veins were empty. Nothing else mattered. He looked down at the puddle of fallen rain near his feet. He could see himself standing: black, terrifying, a reflection.

The streetlights were dim. They made light circles on the sidewalk but not the parking lot near the broken soda machine. He stood in shadows, invisible, only he could see. People passed, but only he could see. Every detail was clear to him at first, but as time passed and his pain grew, things blurred. He fought to see clearly, but it was difficult. People became shapes as the pain grew dryer. He fought to see at first, but as the pain ripped free, the end of the pain was all he wanted. People became things that stood in the way of the end of his waiting. He stood, black, terrifying, a reflection pleased that the clouds had formed above, pleased that the night had grown blacker, pleased that the wait would soon be over.

Something in a pink dress passed, but no, two other things followed. A thing in a Bulls cap and its child passed, but no, a car pulled in behind. He stood, dry, trembling, invisible in the corner behind the soda machine, waiting.

He saw a three piece suit walk out of the station. He glanced around. Nothing followed it. The moment had come. In the pocket of his trench coat was a .38. He drew the pistol and silently approached the thing from behind.

"Give it up, motherfucker," he whispered, pressing the gun against the back of that thing's neck. When he knew it was intimidated, he took three steps back and said, "Don't turn around. Drop your money on the ground and get the fuck away from here."

It said something and that almost made it alive, so "Shut the fuck up," he said. "Just give me the goddam money and get the fuck out of here."

It turned, angry, denied invisibility. A shot was fired.

And he wanted to stop this memory. He wanted to think of nothing, but there was the pain, then thunder.

And he could hear the shot firing. The bullet ripped in, then out, and he could see that three piece suit fall. He could see it fall face first into the water waiting on the sidewalk, face first into the puddle waiting on the sidewalk. He saw its reflection as it fell, he saw its reflection, and it was a man until he only saw water, until he only remembered the water, the water rising as the three piece suit landed, the water falling. His veins were empty, his body dry, and there was only water falling to the ground.

It had fallen on the money. He reached down, pushed it away, took the wallet, the money left the water, the three piece suit in a memory.

The street was clear. No one followed, so he walked to the bridge, as he crossed it, he removed one hundred and thirty-seven dollars from the wallet. The bills were bleeding, but he couldn't care. His veins were empty and there was pain and the pain was about to stop. He stopped, stared out at the river, when he was sure he was invisible again, he tossed the empty wallet and the pistol into the night black water. It was almost over.

The nearest telephone was on the other side of the bridge. When he saw it, he ran searching his pockets for change. He had just enough for a phone call. The booth was lighted and stood apart from the black of the night. As he approached it the light filled him with anticipation. He pulled the door open and stepped into the light. He knew the number by heart. He put the change in the slot and dialed. A phone rang on the other end. When it stopped and he heard a voice, he started talking. "I got a hundred thirty-seven dollars, man, I need some now, I need some now. You gotta meet me, man. You gotta meet me..."

8:55, the rain poured down again, harder than it had fallen all day. The car lot closed, and after a time, the lights dimmed to black. Soon nothing in the alley was visible. He stood in the black, waiting. He could do nothing but wait. The pain was there, stronger. The five-step pit that led to the back door of the Italian restaurant three building back of the alley had flooded to the first step again, but he had to sit down. He wrapped his arms around his stomach, stared at his empty veins, while sitting in a puddle, in a pit, flooded. The rain fell in a continuously intense stream. He stared at the puddles, falling and rising, rising and falling. He wondered if they knew his pain. He wanted them to know his pain.

STRANGER TO MYSELF
Wendy-o Matik

Sometimes I am a stranger to myself, trapped in a house that I do not belong in a neighborhood that bears no warmth or safety in a country that I do not remember on a planet confused with another planet amidst a universe that does not exist. And my life is swallowed up into the void or madness, whichever comes first. It all feels the same, the contradiction of terminology. I disengage, disconnect, dismantle, feed my brain, feed my impulse. The candle stays lit even when there is no fire. The carnival is only a half a block down the road, but she'd rather grind gears in another direction. She's wearing her armor-plated clothes tonight, and the moon feels like a spotlight on her empty soul. The wind sounds like static from a car radio. In the silence she screams. In the silence she cries. In the silence she burns bridges and says goodbye.

EAST 13TH BETWEEN B & C
Terri Weist

There I was, on a fine spring day, walking down 13th, between B and C, toward the park. A yard on the right, welcomed by the littering committee leaving trails of the last time they forgot to listen to their inner ecological child: beer cans, cig butts, fast food chicken nugget containers with the proof right there on the lawn that they had tried all the sauces to douse that fat in. The walkway: a concrete crumble of rocks that lead to the entrance. It was a yard like any other, but leading to two squats. A lot of big metal scraps and junk like that adorned the backyards. Some serious New York style anti-zoo landscaping: damaged, apocalyptic, unfit for your mom, work spaces. Mosaic tiled path, rusted sculptures embraced bald spots of grass like a mother to a soldier on short leave, weird shapes of torched metal sheets covered the front gate.

I'm investigating, just snooping on through and the dogs inside are barking at me and I have to piss. I gape, and a voice intrudes, "Who are YOU looking for?"

"Nobody," I said. How dare he ask. "Just looking."

Then he looked me over with the shaved half of his forehead tilting toward the ground and said, "Do I look like I have a disease?"

I looked directly at him from toe to head, and said, "Maybe... mental..." We said "mental" at the same time. "JINX! OWE ME A COKE... I was just looking around," I said again.

"Oh," he said, lighting something rolled.

"Is that a joint in your hand?"

"Yes," he replied with a pretentious danger in his tone that was supposed to scare me, I guess. It excites me when people try to scare me. I'm always trying to get as close to the edge as I can without falling off, and he was a nut fresh out of the shell. "Do you have some matches? Do you want to smoke it?"

"Maybe," I said, thinking, 'Danger, Will.' "Is this a squat?" I asked.

"Yes," he said, "and we have to go INSIDE to smoke. They'll arrest me." So of course I went inside, and he was happy because he could show those metal forgers next door who broke his windows amidst a six month dispute, still active, that he was his own boss cuz he had this, you know, HOT BITCH with him. All the while I'm thinking to myself, politics, neighbors, sexual assault, danger, limits, and possible witnesses.

Climbing through the backyard of rubble to the terrace of trash, we head through the back room which is dark and narrow, a ten inch passage. Okay, fuck, this guy is some kook, gonna pop me in the head with a jack or try and rope me up while he rapes or pisses on me making me say his ex-boss's name or something equally humiliating... Sick, I know, but don't blame me for what's on TV, okay?

Then he started with the Astrology bit which is okay in some ways, "When were you born, what year? Oh, Chinese New Year, Blah, blah, blah etc...blah, year...?"

"Okay, '63," I said.

"Oh, cat?"

"No, rabbit."

Then he said, "I knew that, but I didn't want to say rabbit because some people get offended and it really could be both, you know, cat and rabbit."

"Oh, right, of course, I could see that," I said. (Right, pal, obviously missing a few stairs on the ol' steps, looney, slightly off kilter, with a storm coming through any second?) I enter his room. Bits of dumpster finds: a wood-burning stove, a bed folded over of damaged goods, broken appliances, lots of ladies clothing hanging from the rafters. Pictures decorate the room, plastered on the wall above the bed plotted out in a sequence of events that weaved and worked its way in to where his state of mind is today right before my eyes.

He tells me, "I shaved my head like this so my neighbor, who smashed the windows I got out of the dumpster and was storing in the courtyard, would think I was crazy. Isn't that a great idea?"

I'm thinking, why does this freak have space heater in surplus, shoes, pantyhose, and several suitcases of women's clothing all over the room? He is a mass murderer. I bet he's psycho and is just pulling some 'insane mellow guy' thing with me. I bet he hangs out at the bus depot and waits for them to get out, startled, and lures them (tourists, business types), takes their stuff. He's holed up in this place, on the run from the Man. There are so many people in New York it's not that difficult. This is a thinking man, I thought. I asked him if he got his electricity from the city street. He said, "Yeah," with an air of false accomplishment. He was the best dressed squatter I had never seen, I guess with all the women's clothing over all the fucking place. He was spruced up in rolled-up khakis, a button-down blue cotton shirt with a necktie, one of those knit ones from Uruguay, he said, that's where he was from.

I'm thinking about asking him who the people on the walls are—his family or an imaginary family? Was he the lost 'family man' Henry Rollins sang to us about with conviction and bloody vocal chords long before I saw him walking down Madison Avenue? At first I wasn't sure whether to believe him because I've dealt with multiple personalities before, no novice to schizophrenia here. Some folks actually fantasize with more life than reality itself. Weighing these possibilities, I could see he was for real, a live kook dwelling in the building for three years. He left Boston, his job selling jewelry, a wife and three kids who are there in the photo: two boys, one girl. He was a jeweler and his friends want to send him back to Uruguay because, "They think," he said, "I'm losing my marbles... Do you?"

"Of course not," I lied, taking my last hit off the dirtweed bobe. In one photo he is sitting on the beach with his lovely wife, whom he loves very much and misses.

"That photo is from Florida. We were on vacation, at the beach one day." The caption has their names and the title read, 'Stormy Lovers, On The Beach' with these huge storm clouds in the back. Talk about torture. "My wife said, 'How did they know?' "

Here we have the complete story of the past, the wall of photos, some he's found recently mixed in with sentimentality to lighten the place up. There was drywall that had been punched, I might add.

Here we have a man stripped of all power, all responsibility and reason, cowering in the immediate denial of 'power figure'. Here we have a masked reality with pictures of happy family covering drywall, well insulating a body that three times created, three times split, 50% bailed. Sounds like home to me. Now a zero, hero.

The unborn virgin. The unwound, once tightly wound asshole. A Virgo so puritanical, and industrious as he was saying, he can't see his way out of the paper bag black hole that will someday be an artists' loft, cafe, barf, or some rip-off artfuck overpriced dwelling. Now it's free. "Do you write to them?" I ask.

"No," he says regretfully, staring at the photocopy hanging on the wall. " 'Stormy Lovers,' she said, 'How did they know?' "

My mind switches channels to 'Gee, Batman, do you think he assaulted her?' 'Could be, Robin, could be...' Below that, a letter she wrote to him, trickling down the chalky drywall like a gold digger's map of treasures; below that, a letter from his wife's lawyer filing for divorce.

Not much to figure out. Who knows? This guy is insane, but by who's sanity meter? He just got the hell out of Dodge and repeated what a terrible man he was. It's not easy being a man these days, everyone hip to the fact that you're a pig. He seems to really love her. What does that have to do with anything? What does self-destruction and heartbreak have to do with losing your mind? Even chemical imbalances seem more noticeable and less surprising among individuals these days. Maybe it's a sign of the times... Being a killer is a sign of these times also, maybe he is.

Took the women with their suitcases back to his place.

I try to convince him that his friends could be right about going back to Uruguay. The United States is crazy, man. He stares at the floor, shaking his head and laughing, "No way! I will not go back... yet." He lost his mind in crazy America. He learned to enjoy scaring people. In deep sheep. Trying the luck of the lamb.

Nobody can be certain of when the cards will fall dead, stacked against you. You never do really know for sure whether or not you're talking to a crazy man. He took off his clothes and put on all white, a priest's collar, white pants, and shoes and an ecru knit tie. "I am the white priest," he said.

I knew it was time to go. Besides it was starting to get dark. "Okay, well, ah, I gotta go, my friends are waiting for me. Goodbye!" He quickly walked behind me, begging me to stay.

"No, sorry, man. I gotta split," I said with a tone that really meant 'Don't fuck with me, you freak, I'll spear you!' I got to the sidewalk, opened the gate, mumbled "See Ya," and quickly bolted with my head jumping around like it was just blown out with too much wasabi mustard. Stoned, thinking, 'That was close!'

All that just for some adventure and some bobe. We're bored white youth looking for kicks. No, I didn't see any crack pipes in there. But he did mention something about anarchy and how he just couldn't go back to that other life. Not now. No way.

REPORTAGE
Jack Hirschman

I'm sitting in the Caffe Trieste talking
to a friend when a man standing at the open
front door yells in, "Anybody owns a motorcycle
it's being ticketed by the cops."

The entire cafe suddenly exudes an ether
of fear, a heightened almost glittering
terror paralyzing everyone in his or her place.

It's like some paranoidal cocaine or semi-
radiant landscape revealed at the top of
one's song in a wobbling saloon at night;
only it's daytime, and it's fear now,

law'n'order fear totally here at the raising
of voice; it's released, no question about it,
the barrel of the human mouth is aimed

at human rage, and lying everywhere in wait:
the police state.

INFORMATION O.D.
Lisa Radon

september 24th was my father's birthday
i would not have known this
if my sister had not told me on september 21st
that september 24th was my father's birthday

on september 24th i was standing in a BART station at 5:53 p.m.
looking up at the data flowing by on the overhead
a news item about brian boytano and debi thomas
i was outraged to realize that i knew that these two were ice skaters
i know who these obscure athletes are
and i can't remember my father's birthday
i can't believe that precious space in my brain
is used up by this useless piece of trivia
that by occupying space in my brain
it is preventing the storage of other essential data

there is so much to know
and so much i keep forgetting

i'm trying to stay away from the easiest to input sources of data
these include television, radio, newspapers, magazines,
toothpaste tubes, cereal boxes, muni posters

there is so much to know
and so much i keep forgetting
i fear i am reaching maximum storage potential
that overload is imminent

i don't know
i can't remember
e, none of the above?
i'm not sure
i can't quite recall
i don't think so
where have i seen you before?
don't i know you?
i don't know

can't shut it off
can't close the doors of my ears, my eyes
can't stop the input, INPUT, MORE INPUT
i don't remember
input, process, store, cross-reference, input, retrieve
i can't...
input, more data, more data
warning, overload, system error,
i...i...
552-67-6813
C2315416
kingdom, phylum, class, order, family, genus, species
wan that aprille with is sure sota...
255-8830, 659-4565,
cogito ergo sum
the choice of a new generation
BLUE!

1492, 1776, 1812
i pledge allegiance to the flag...
Albany!
the square root of 81 is 9
bush, reagan, carter, ford, nixon, johnson, kennedy
tastes just like chicken
Charles Phillip Arthur George
can you tell me how to get, how to get to sesame street...
call now, operators are standing by
uno, dos, tres...
radon
atomic number: 86.
atomic weight: 222.
o, i wish i was an oscar mayer wiener...
"love is not love which alters when it alteration finds
nor bends with the remover to remove"
heads shoulders knees and toes, knees and toes...
my name is lisa elena radon. born 4/5/66, carmel, california. homo
sapien. biped. omnivore.
i'm sorry, what was the question?

and when i am very old
i will no doubt be the one you will see on street corners, at bus stops
mumbling apparent nonsense
while my head lolls from side to side
helplessly regurgitating decades of input

ENDANGERED SPECIES
Jennifer Joseph

In the beginning were edible noodle letters filling blue bowls of salty soup, carrot cubes and soggy celery, limp letters spelling out simple words in a huge shallow spoon—soon recognition triggered curiosity, swallowing wiggling words in one gulp whistling down the gullet (and oh, the holes in those o's of spaghetti-o's and cheerio's) carefully reading the brightly-colored backs of cereal boxes, reaching to the box bottom for a prize wrapped in plastic—cutting a cardboard Jackson 5 single from the back of a box of Alpha-bits

Sudden fascination with multisyllabic anthropomorphic linguistics learning the biggest word the English language had to offer—28 solid letters of antidisestablishmentarianism—too large for a scrambled scrabble board— suddenly See Spot Run had nothing on Green Eggs and Ham starving for knowledge voraciously reading everything in sight: street signs, headlines, golden realm of intimate imagination, mining the golden veins of distant mind travel and adventure, reading by flashlight every night under the covers after bedtime, now still the phone rings "Did I wake you up?" "No I'm reading, what do you want?" Enjoying the easy silent grace of fictional characters more than people present in person preferring fiction where problems are resolved by page 274; fiction: a place where endings end—instead of real life which just goes on regardless

Books are such precious objects I think staring at Sumerian stones carefully carved by craftsmen in 5000 B.C.—the library at Alexandria one of the wonders of the ancient world burned to the ground with literature lost forever lighting up the night sky—oh well no crisis there—illuminated manuscripts meticulously copied by medieval monks—no dark-robed monks now just today's tattooed teenagers with all of the illumination and none of the manuscripts—Bucky teaches a high school creative writing class, asks the students to describe something—anything—they can't do it, don't have access to language, can't find the words, everything's been shown and told, they say "I like it." "What do you like about it?" he asks "I dunno. I just like it." Nowadays the dancing electron screen does all the talking, we're just passive observers laughing at the funny parts and reaching for the remote

When VCRs came into vogue they said no one would go to the movies anymore when fax machines were invented they were ready to write off bike messengers and federal express, sure there's a phenomenon known as planned obsolescence, a technological reference, look at recorded music: thick plates of 78s, 7-inch singles, cassette tapes, LPs, CDs—has it changed the way we hear music? or is it just this year's consumer-driven shark frenzy of capitalistic opportunistic Darwinian theories at work? there'll always be new system software, version upgrades, a faster modem, bigger memory in a smaller microchip, bigger better faster more—will there ever be a better poem than the Odyssey by Homer (who goes by one name like Prince and Madonna)? if there is a better poem will anyone be around for 2500 years to acknowledge its lasting power? will it be a better poem because it's on CD-ROM? maybe a faster poem, maybe a louder poem, but no, not necessarily a better poem

That's it, it's over, pack your bags and move to Mars, lower the flag and go down with the ship, it's over, a done deal, can't stop the plow of progress, can't halt the march of time— true predictions, inquiring minds want to know—just ask those bestselling authors, stars of the american airwaves: Howard Stern, Rush Limbaugh, Jerry Seinfeld, hello? sure anyone can write a book but can you sell it without a TV show? and what's wrong with reading for pleasure's sake?

I read books when I *don't* want to be interactive—I spend more than enough time with the phone/fax/copier/computer/answering machine/ meowing cat/noisy washing machine/humming refrigerator/radio/TV/ my problems/your problems—I spend enough time interacting—quiet time is what I crave, can never have enough of—just me and my book, heavy in hand, crisp smell of new ink, crack of the spine, ssshhh quiet— pages turning–ssshhh listen it's the sound of an active imagination churning

THE FRESH AIR OF HOPE
K.L. Hill

I have said
That I don't really
Expect things to get
Any better in my lifetime,
When there are so many
Left-over people
In this generation
Who seem beyond recovery,
Living out of shopping carts
Loaded up with left-over
Cans and bottles
To cash in for small change
That's not enough
For a cheap room.

And I have said
That it would take more
Than a new president
with good intentions
And the high hopes
Of a few tough women
In the senate
To get the hunger
Off the streets,
And the blood and the fire
Off the streets.

But what would I say
To offer encouragement,
When the hard reality
Of opposition
Surrounds you,
Sniping at every effort,
From the doorways
And the corridors
Of the status quo?

I should say
That I would struggle
To overcome
The cynic in me,
To offer words of support
For those who have promised
To work hard, trying
To clean up the mess
That was left behind
By the power
Of me-first money
That has gone too far.

And I should say
That there are many
Who have touched you

From the curbsides,
And at your doorstep,
And many more
Who were touched

By the fresh air of hope
That flows
Through your open door,
And I've never heard
So many marching bands
Sound so bright,
As they passed
In review for you.

And I should say,
Please don't forget to keep
Your doors and windows
Thrown open,
And to keep your ear
Tuned in to the music
Of the streets,
And that sometimes
It's a good thing
To go out
On the back porch,
Late at night,
When you don't think
Anyone is listening,
And blow a few choruses
Of some good old B flat
Twelve bar blues,
And that sometimes
It's a good thing
To try something
In a new key,
Just to see
If you can work it out.

Contributors' Notes

SUE A. AUSTIN lives in Michigan.

DAN ARCHIBALD is from Illinois.

MARCI BLACKMAN co-edited the queer anthology, *Beyond Definition*.

DAN BUSKIRK most recently runs a record shop in San Francisco

MICHELE C. is the author of *Solitary Traveler*.

BUZZ CALLAWAY has a novel out called *Specimen Tank*.

CAROL CAVILEER is the author of *Feminine Resistance*.

ANN CHERNOW lives in Connecticut.

AARON COMETBUS has published the much-loved zine, *Ride the Whol Whip Cometbus*, for ten years.

JOIE COOK is the author of several chapbooks, including *Acts of Submission*.

ELI COPPOLA has written several books, including *The Animals We Keep In The City*.

NANCY DEPPER has written several chapbooks, including *Bodies of Work*, and was a member of the 1993 San Francisco Poetry Slam team.

KEITH DODSON publishes a zine called *The Guts-ette*.

DEBBIE DRECHSLER's comix have appeared in many publications, including *Blab* and *Drawn and Quarterly*.

MARY FLEENER's work has appeared in many places, and her comic book is called *Slutburger*.

FLY is a New York City artist, contactable via Gargoyle Mechanique Lab.

STEPHEN FOWLER is a playwright and author.

KATHI GEORGES is director of the Marilyn Monroe Memorial Theater in San Francisco.

CHRISTIEN GHOLSON lives in Iowa.

EVE GILBERT writes and draws the comic book *Dangerous Pussy*.

FRED GREEN eats meat and lives in Florida.

DYLAN HALBERG lives in Southern California.

TREBOR HEALEY co-edited the queer literary anthology, *Beyond Definition*.

K.L. HILL often reads his writing at poetry readings in San Francisco.

BLACKY HIX's work has appeared in numerous zines. He's originally from Oklahoma.

JACK HIRSCHMAN is the author of many books, including *Endless Threshold*.

ROBERT HOWINGTON lives in Texas and is editor and publisher of Homemade Ice Cream Press.

ALBERT HUFFSTICKLER's writing can be found in many small press publications. He lives in Texas.

AYN IMPERATO writes a column for *Maximum Rock'n'Roll*, and is editor and publisher at Andromeda Press.

BRUCE ISAACSON is editor and publisher of Zeitgeist Press books.

BRUCE JACKSON lives in California.

DAVID JEWELL lives in Texas and is the author of several books including *Lizards Again*.

DARRIN JOHNSON lives in Washington.

JENNIFER JOSEPH is editor and publisher of Manic D Press books.

VAMPYRE MIKE KASSEL has written several books, including *Graveyard Golf and other stories*.

KEITH KNIGHT's comic, *The K Chronicles*, is featured in the *SF Weekly*.

DEAN KUIPERS is most recently managing editor of *Huh* magazine.

M. KYLE & L. ANGELESCO, writer and artist respectively, are co-authors of the comic book, *Wenches & Wrenches*.

SPARROW 13 LAUGHINGWAND is the author of several chapbooks including *Bums Eat Shit and other poems*.

JON LONGHI's most recent book is *The Rise and Fall of Third Leg*.

JEFFREY MCDANIEL toured as a Spoken Word performer with the Lollapalooza Festival. He is the author of *Alibi School*.

MABEL MANEY is an artist and author of several books including *The Case of the Not-So-Nice Nurse*, and *The Case of the Good-For-Nothing Girlfriend*.

WENDY-O MATIK is the author of *Love Like Rage*.

RIBA MERYL lives in Southern California.

JERRY D. MILEY 's poem originally appeared in his book, *Standing In Line*.

ALICE OLDS-ELLINGSON lives in Oregon. She is the author of *The Devil Won't Let Me In*.

MARC OLMSTED lives in Northern California, and has a book, *Milky Desire*.

STEVEN DEAN PASTIS is from Southern California.

ANN PETERS lives in Utah.

LISA RADON is the mother of Oscar, and author of *Now Hear This*.

RICHARD SALA is an artist and author of several books including *Hypnotic Tales* and *Black Cat Crossing*.

ISABEL SAMARAS is an artist currently living in Northern California.

PRISCILLA SEARS recently saw her work, *All Purpose Valentine*, performed at the American Stage Festival in New Hampshire.

SHAYNO lives in San Francisco and does a zine called *Comatoast*.

BILL SHIELDS is the author of *Human Shrapnel* and *The South East Asian Book of the Dead*.

LYNDA S. SILVA lives in Southern California.

BUCKY SINISTER's new book, *King of the Roadkills*, will be available soon.

HAL SIROWITZ has read his work on MTV, and performs often at the Nuyorican Poets Cafe in New York City.

DASHKA SLATER's writing appears regularly in the *East Bay Express*.

JUSTIN SPRING lives in Florida.

W.H.STEIGERWALDT's work appears in zines. He lives in Wisconsin.

KIMBERLY STRANDBERG is from Massachusetts.

KIMI SUGIOKA is the author of *The Language of Birds*.

LISA TAPLIN raises lizards and is assistant editor at Manic D Press.

MICHELLE TEA is the author of many chapbooks and personal zines.

ADRIAN TOMINE's mini-comic is called *Optic Nerve*.

CAROLE VINCENT lives in Oregon, and has been published by Dead Angel Press.

VIOLET is currently working on a novel in San Francisco.

TERRI WEIST is the author of *Jesus Sister*.

DAVID WEST has written several books, including *Elegy For The Old Stud*.

GERALD WILLIAMS lives in New Jersey.

DANIELLE WILLIS is the author of *Dogs In Lingerie,* and received rave reviews for her one-woman show, *Breakfast In The Flesh District.*

BANA WITT is the author of four books, including *Mobius Stripper.*

KURT ZAPATA's story originally appeared in his book of short stories, *Back on the Swing Shift.*

manic d press
publications

Beyond Definition. *Marci Blackman & Trebor Healey, editors* $10.95 ISBN 0-916397-30-0
The Rise and Fall of Third Leg. *Jon Longhi* $9.95 ISBN 0-916397-27-0
Specimen Tank. *Buzz Callaway* $10.95 ISBN 0-916397-20-3
The Verdict Is In. *edited by Kathi Georges & Jennifer Joseph.* $9.95 ISBN 0-916397-25-4
The Roots of a Thousand Embraces. *Juan Felipe Herrera* $7.00 ISBN 0-916397-28-9
Love Like Rage. *Wendy-o Matik.* $7.00 ISBN 0-916397-30-0 ISBN 0-916397-31-9
The Language of Birds. *Kimi Sugioka.* $7.00 ISBN 0-916397-32-7
Elegy for the Old Stud. *David West.* $7.00 ISBN 0-916397-26-2
The Back of a Spoon. *Jack Hirschman.* $7.00 ISBN 0-916397-22-X
Mobius Stripper. *Bana Witt.* $8.00 ISBN 0-916397-23-8
Baroque Outhouse/The Decapitated Head of a Dog. *Randolph Nae.*$7.00 ISBN 0-916397-16-5
Graveyard Golf and other stories. *Vampyre Mike Kassel.* $7.00 ISBN 0-916397-15-7
Bricks and Anchors. *Jon Longhi.* $8.00 ISBN 0-916397-12-2
The Devil Won't Let Me In. *Alice Olds-Ellingson.* $7.95 ISBN 0-916397-11-4
Greatest Hits. *edited by Jennifer Joseph.* $7.00 ISBN 0-916397-03-3
Lizards Again. *David Jewell.* $7.00 ISBN 0-916397-01-7
The Future Isn't What It Used To Be. *Jennifer Joseph.* $7.00 ISBN 0-916397-00-9
Acts of Submission. *Joie Cook.* $4.00 ISBN 0-916397-04-1
12 Bowls of Glass. *Bucky Sinister.* $3.00 ISBN 0-916397-06-8
Zucchini and other stories. *Jon Longhi.* $3.00 ISBN 0-916397-07-6
Standing In Line. *Jerry D. Miley.* $3.00 ISBN 0-916397-08-4
Drugs. *Jennifer Joseph.* $3.00 ISBN 0-916397-09-2
Bums Eat Shit and other poems. *Sparrow 13 LaughingWand.* $3.00 ISBN 0-916397-05-X
Into The Outer World. *David Jewell.* $3.00 ISBN 0-916397-14-9
Asphalt Rivers. *Bucky Sinister.* $3.00 ISBN 0-916397-19-X
Solitary Traveler. *Michele C.* $3.00 ISBN 0-916397-13-0
Night Is Colder Than Autumn. *Jerry D. Miley.* $3.00 ISBN 0-916397-18-1
Seven Dollar Shoes. *Sparrow 13 Laughing Wand.* $3.00 ISBN 0-916397-24-6
Intertwine. *Jennifer Joseph.* $3.00 ISBN 0-916397-33-5
Feminine Resistance. *Carol Cavileer.* $3.00 ISBN 0-916397-35-1
Now Hear This. *Lisa Radon.* $3.00 ISBN 0-916397-36-X
Bodies of Work. *Nancy Depper.* $3.00 ISBN 0-916397-34-3
Corazon Del Barrio. *Jorge Argueta.* $4.00 ISBN 0-916397-29-7

To order, please send your name and address with a check or
money order (include $2.00 for postage and handling) to:

**manic d press
p.o. box 410804
san francisco ca 94141 usa**
send $1 for complete catalog

bookstores and libraries:
please place orders with publishers group west